The Rest Is Silence . . .

Everyone in the saloon had fallen silent. Now they began whispering, eyes darting toward Slocum and then away if he tried to look directly at them. This would be talked about for days to come. Life was pretty dull in Grizzly Flats.

Beefsteak made a point of ignoring him, too, making Slocum even more curious. He touched his Colt Navy, then went to the swinging doors and looked out into the rain. White chunks of sleet mixed with the rain, preventing him from seeing as far as across the broad main street that meandered through the middle of town.

Slocum stepped out and knew instantly he was exposed to more than a late autumn storm. He heard boots scraping on the boardwalk to his right. Without hesitation, he half turned, hand flashing to the butt of his six-shooter. He drew, aimed, and fired just as the gunman cleared leather. Slocum's slug ripped through the man's belly, doubling him over. He staggered, went to one knee, and tried to raise his pistol. Slocum fired again.

The reports came as one. The man's round went wide of Slocum's head and was swallowed in the rain. Slocum's cut through the brim of the man's hat and plowed into his forehead.

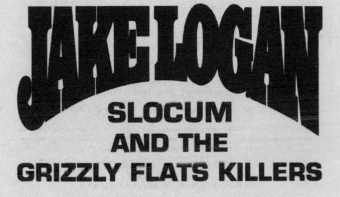

JAKE LOGAN

SLOCUM
AND THE
GRIZZLY FLATS KILLERS

JOVE BOOKS, NEW YORK

THE BERKLEY PUBLISHING GROUP
Published by the Penguin Group
Penguin Group (USA) Inc.
375 Hudson Street, New York, New York 10014, USA

Penguin Group (Canada), 90 Eglinton Avenue East, Suite 700, Toronto, Ontario M4P 2Y3, Canada (a division of Pearson Penguin Canada Inc.) • Penguin Books Ltd., 80 Strand, London WC2R 0RL, England • Penguin Group Ireland, 25 St. Stephen's Green, Dublin 2, Ireland (a division of Penguin Books Ltd.) • Penguin Group (Australia), 707 Collins Street, Melbourne, Victoria 3008, Australia (a division of Pearson Australia Group Pty. Ltd.) • Penguin Books India Pvt. Ltd., 11 Community Centre, Panchsheel Park, New Delhi—110 017, India • Penguin Group (NZ), 67 Apollo Drive, Rosedale, Auckland 0632, New Zealand (a division of Pearson New Zealand Ltd.) • Penguin Books (South Africa) (Pty.) Ltd., Rosebank Office Park, 181 Jan Smuts Avenue, Parktown North 2193, South Africa • Penguin China, B7 Jiaming Center, 27 East Third Ring Road North, Chaoyang District, Beijing 100020, China

Penguin Books Ltd., Registered Offices: 80 Strand, London WC2R 0RL, England

This is a work of fiction. Names, characters, places, and incidents either are the product of the author's imagination or are used fictitiously, and any resemblance to actual persons, living or dead, business establishments, events, or locales is entirely coincidental.

SLOCUM AND THE GRIZZLY FLATS KILLERS

A Jove Book / published by arrangement with the author

PUBLISHING HISTORY
Jove edition / February 2013

Copyright © 2013 by Penguin Group (USA) Inc.
Cover illustration by Sergio Giovine.

ISBN: 978-0-515-15310-1

JOVE®
Jove Books are published by The Berkley Publishing Group, a division of Penguin Group (USA) Inc., 375 Hudson Street, New York, New York 10014. JOVE® is a registered trademark of Penguin Group (USA) Inc. The "J" design is a trademark of Penguin Group (USA) Inc.

PRINTED IN THE UNITED STATES OF AMERICA

10 9 8 7 6 5 4 3 2 1

ALWAYS LEARNING   **PEARSON**

1

"You shouldn't have left camp," Isaac Comstock said, looking around nervously. The wind whistled through Spring Canyon, which Mirabelle Comstock had followed to reach him. A hint of freezing rain touched the air with an icy threat, and the tallest peaks of the Sierras to the east were well dressed with late autumn snow.

Mount Pleasant to the west mocked him. Since he and the others had trooped the twenty-five miles from Placerville into these godforsaken mountains, the landmarks they sought had eluded them.

"You don't have to be so jumpy, Ike," the tall, well-built woman said, tucking a strand of her soft chestnut hair back under her bonnet. "They don't know I came lookin' for you. Why do they care anyway? Aren't we all out here for the same goldanged reason?"

"'Spect so, Mira, 'spect so," Comstock said, "but you know how Terrence gets."

"His ass is a real tight vise is the way you said it last night."

"Don't talk like that," he said sharply. "That's not proper."

"For a woman, you mean. Ike, darling, I do more 'n just fix food. I listen. I know you don't trust him. Why not?"

"How do you think he found out about the gold in the first place?"

"I wondered, but there are always maps floating about. Sacramento has so many old prospectors selling maps, you stumble over them on the way to market."

"I wouldn't have put up our bottom dollar for anything like that."

"That's just one reason I love you so," she said. She put down the basket with its red-and-white-checked napkin covering the contents and stepped closer to throw her arms around his neck. "I'd walk through hell barefoot for you 'cuz you're 'bout the most sensible man I've ever known. There has to be something to Terrence's claims or you wouldn't have drug me along out here into nowhere."

"I hope so." He held her but craned around to see if anyone came along the canyon trail.

"What's eatin' you so?" She pushed back and saw her husband lick his lips nervously.

"I thought this might be a wild-goose chase until . . ."

She looked at him sharply. Her usually soft chocolate eyes took on a hardness that speared him where he stood.

"What do you mean?"

"I worried this wouldn't amount to anything, and we'd lose that seventeen dollars I gave over to Terrence."

"You *worried*," she said pointedly. "You're not worryin' any longer? What have you found?"

He wiped a grimy hand over his chapped lips, then looked around as if someone could overhear. As far as Mirabelle knew, there wasn't another living human within two miles—the distance back to camp where she had left two other women and that good-for-nothing Lucas Sennick. He did nothing to uphold his share of the work and hadn't spent ten minutes looking for the cache with the other men. Between Ike, Terrence, and David Garrison, they had covered many miles of the eastern California country in the past week. Garrison had even offered to drive into Grizzly Flats for supplies when Sennick had complained about a bad back and how the wagon hitting potholes and rocks in the road hurt him something fierce. If it hadn't been for Terrence and Ike laying down the law, Sennick would have dodged even that simple chore.

He had taken longer than he should have covering the few miles into town, and Mirabelle was sure she smelled liquor on the man's breath when he returned, showing he had dawdled just to get out of trooping through the hills. He'd want his share when they found the hidden gold, but he wouldn't do a damned thing to help them.

"What have you found?" Her breath came faster and her vision blurred a mite. They were going to be rich!

"Not the cache but proof there's something to the story." Comstock pushed back his coat and fished around in his vest pocket. He drew something out and held it in his closed fist.

"Show me!"

"You have to pay me first," he said, grinning broadly.

She grabbed him by his jug ears, pulled his face to hers, and kissed him soundly. The kiss would have gone on longer except that he opened his hand. The wan sunlight glinted off a pair of gold coins.

Mirabelle let out a whoop of glee.

"You found them!"

"No, no, wait. I told you. I didn't find the cache, just these two coins. But I reckon they was dropped. That means the hiding place is around here somewhere close."

She involuntarily looked about. The terrain was mountainous and so rugged that climbing any of the peaks would shred the leather off a man's boot soles. But she thought hard for a moment before speaking.

"They wouldn't have gone too high into the hills. There likely wasn't time. They found a cave? A petered-out mine? This place has old mines everywhere."

"The gold played out in the early fifties," Comstock said. He looked toward Baltic Peak to the north and shivered. Mirabelle knew why. They had spent days there and had almost died from exposure. "But that don't mean there can't be gold stuffed in after the miners left."

"Why're you so edgy, Ike? This is good news!" She looked at him. He hadn't shaved in a week and the stubble was turning into a beard. For the first time she noticed it was shot with gray strands. "You're worrying yourself into an early grave."

"I . . . what if we don't tell the rest, Mira? What if we find the gold and then keep it all for ourselves?"

She stared at him with wide eyes. This wasn't the man she knew. Isaac Comstock was as honest as the day was long, though there might be some question about finding stolen gold and keeping it. But it had been years. Anyone with a claim to the gold was long gone, except Wells Fargo, and what did that company need with the gold? They'd already settled any claims. Likely, some vice president in a fancy pinstripe suit would keep the gold for himself and cheat his employer. The money sat better in their pocket than joining a ton more of gold in some San Francisco bank vault.

"That wouldn't be right."

Comstock hung his shaggy head, then nodded. He didn't say a word.

"We ought to get back to camp and let the others know. That was the idea, wasn't it? If enough of us came out, we could find the gold before winter set in with a vengeance. There's a powerful lot of land to search, even if you know it's somewhere near."

"If'n you only found the two coins, the train robbers might have dropped them as they rode through on their way to the real hidin' place."

Comstock swiped at his mouth again and nodded once more. She had no idea what was going through her husband's head. She thought she knew him as well as any woman could know her man, but now she was beginning to wonder. The lure of riches crushed any morality in him. He was willing to cheat his partners, and she knew it wasn't just for her. Isaac Comstock wanted the gold for what it would buy for Isaac Comstock.

"We can eat, then go back," she said. "I brought enough for both of us. A picnic."

Comstock took a deep breath, squared his shoulders, and said, "Ain't right. Let's tell the others. It's gonna be close to sundown when we get back, and these ain't hills to be roamin' in after dark."

"You see any bear spoor?"

"Some. They're eating anything they can before hibernation. That makes 'em mighty dangerous."

"You want to leave the basket for them?" Mirabelle was happy to see this brought forth a smile, then a laugh.

"We can eat while we walk. It'd be a shame to waste whatever you fixed up all special for me on some grizzly bear."

"I don't know," she said, hanging on to his arm and putting her head on his shoulder. "I'm kinda fond of this grizzly bear."

He favored her with a growl deep in his throat. They both laughed and started back for their camp at the mouth of Spring Canyon.

"I'm remembering landmarks so I can find this place again."

Mirabelle looked around but saw nothing extraordinary.

"I found the coins just around the bend in this canyon. There was a strange trio of peaks. Finding the bend is going to be the problem since there are so many branching canyons."

They trooped along. Mirabelle fished out some corn bread and handed a piece to Ike. She added a piece of greasy rabbit that Clay Terrence had bagged that morning. Sennick had been responsible for cooking it while the women worked to wash clothing, and he had let the meat char. It still tasted good after having next to nothing for a few days. Nobody wanted to send Sennick back into town to fetch more flour and bacon. Money was running low and he might decide to spend what little they had on whiskey.

"Wait, Ike. Isn't camp down this branch of the canyon?" She stooped and looked around. The sun had already dipped behind the tallest peak to the west, turning the landscape into a strange, alien terrain she didn't—quite—remember.

"It's easy to get lost in the maze. Camp's that way."

Before she could ask if he was sure, an ear-piercing shriek echoed down the canyon from the direction Ike had indicated. They looked at each other. He touched the Smith & Wesson tucked into his waistband.

"What can that be?" She worried that some animal was being tortured. When another cry came, she worried that it wasn't an animal. It sounded too human.

And then the cries stopped. The silence was somehow worse than the cries of agony.

"You stay here," he said, drawing the pistol from his belt.

"No, Ike, don't. You can't barge in. There's no telling what's happening."

"I got to find out."

Mirabelle tried to make sense of the new sounds coming from the direction of their campsite and couldn't. Ike obviously deciphered the noises. He blanched under the suntan and grime on his face.

"Ike!" She grabbed his arm and dug in her fingernails to hold him back. "You go bargin' in now knowin' what's happenin' and you'll end up in a world of misery."

A gunshot decided the issue.

He jerked free, cocked his pistol, and shoved her away.

"Stay put. I mean it, Mira." With that, he stalked off.

She watched him disappear into the gathering twilight. Her heart hammered fiercely. She clamped her eyes shut and hugged herself when she heard sounds—female sounds—from the camp. She couldn't tell if it was Irene or Cara. And it didn't matter. She knew one of the other women was being raped.

Her eyes came open like a window blind snapping up when another gunshot sounded. She looked around, found a rock at her feet with a sharp edge. Picking it up and swinging it around, she knew it made a good axe head. She didn't have time to lash it to a shaft. She'd have to clutch it in her hands. Already sweaty palms turned the piece of sharp-edged flint slippery. Or was it blood? She opened her hand and saw thin trickles of blood as black as night oozing from cuts where she had gripped the rock too hard.

Another gunshot

She rushed after her husband. There wasn't anything else she could do. Standing by and hearing the horrible sounds of carnage tore her up inside. Her imagination might be worse than the actual, but she doubted it. She heard more sounds of cloth tearing and a woman begging for mercy. The words were muffled so much she couldn't recognize who was pleading. Somehow, she thought it was Cara. She liked her more than Irene and hoped she was still alive.

Mirabelle worried she would miss the camp and blunder into the middle of the massacre in the dark. Indians? They hadn't heard of any predations. The tribes in the area were mostly content to farm, not like the savages in New Mexico and Arizona Territories. But if not Indians, then who?

"Drop that gun!" She recognized Ike's voice and turned toward it. His sense of direction in the dark was better than hers. He was dozens of yards to her right.

"Here's another one!"

She didn't recognize that voice or the others joining in. Then any hope of identification disappeared in a flurry of gunshots. Long tongues of orange flame lanced though the dark. She clutched her crude war axe and made her way toward the fight.

"Dammit," a man cried. "He winged me!"

"Keep your damn fool head down. We'll take care of him. He can't have much ammo."

"They didn't have a hundred rounds to start," piped up another.

Mirabelle saw the eye-dazzling streaks of gunfire and how they converged even farther to her right. She made out Ike's silhouette. He stood exposed, his six-shooter held at the end of a stiff arm. Swinging back and forth, he sought a decent target. He fired twice, and then the outlaws in the camp homed in on him. She cried out as he jerked about. Ike dropped his gun. When it hit the ground, it discharged.

But he didn't care. Isaac Comstock sank to his knees, clutching his chest.

Three dark forms moved closer. All three men fired at the same time, ending Comstock's life. He flopped onto the ground and didn't move. That didn't stop them from emptying their six-guns into him.

"We ought to have left one of them alive."

"We couldn't get nuthin' out of the one we questioned. I mean, we asked him all nice and polite and he wouldn't tell us nuthin' but lies."

"He surely did spin a different tale from the one he told in town," said another hidden man. His laugh was cold and evil.

"What's that?"

The third man silenced the other two.

Mirabelle thought they had heard her outcry or the pounding of her heart as it tried to jump from her chest. She took a better grip on the hand axe, ready to kill them all for what they had done.

To her relief, they moved away, fanning out and fading into the dark.

She started to go to her husband. There might be a spark of life left in him she could nurture and build back into the life he had once enjoyed. Before she could get to the camp, more gunfire rang out. She dropped her hand axe and clapped bloody hands over her ears in a vain attempt to block out the sound. She failed.

"Got him. Only nicked him in the leg."

"That'll keep him from runnin' like the other tried."

She recognized Terrence's voice immediately as he cursed his captors. They dragged him back into camp and dropped him to the ground by the guttering campfire.

"Let's get some heat. Put a few pieces of wood on the fire."

One man obeyed, and the flames shot skyward. The sudden light blinded her for a moment or she might have gotten a better look at the attackers. Then all she could see was Terrence being held so his hand was near the fire.

"Why not tell us where the gold is?"

"Go to hell," Terrence grated out. Then he screamed when they forced his hand into the fire. The sizzle and pop sickened Mirabelle. Then she had to put her hand over her mouth and nose as the stench of burned human flesh drifted down on the night wind to her.

"Try the other hand. They're gonna call you Stumpy, if they call you anything at all," warned an outlaw, the one she thought was the leader.

Terrence screamed again as they burned his other hand.

"What we're askin' ain't worth the pain. You can always find more gold—if you're alive to do the huntin'. Where's the gold hid?"

"I don't know. We ain't found it!"

"Now, that's not what your late and prob'ly unlamented friend had to say. He was boastin' how you folks had found your weight in gold. We reckoned by now you were loadin' it into that broke-down wagon of yours."

"Not find it. No gold," Terrence sobbed out.

"This was a right nice campsite you had. Homey. But we might be persuaded into givin' you a share of the gold if you tell us where it is."

Mirabelle knew the lie instantly. So did Terrence. He cursed them until they set fire to his coat—while he was still wearing it. The man ran about slapping at the flames, but the fire had found a home in the greasy cloth. He burned like a pitch torch.

"Shoot me, please, oh, God, the pain!"

"Be glad to put you out of your misery if you'll tell us where the gold is." Again that uncaring laughter.

Terrence died before he could think up a lie.

"Shit. We done kilt all of 'em and there's no sign of the gold anywhere."

"We got 'em all?" asked one.

"Think so. Two women, four men." The outlaw speaking paused. "Wish there was another woman. I didn't get my chance with either of them others."

"Go jerk off. It's better than anything I got out of mine."

Mirabelle felt woozy and sank down to hands and knees. She ought to run but couldn't find the strength. The men rummaged through camp for another twenty minutes hunting for a map or gold or anything that might show that the gold had even been found.

She pressed her fingers against the two gold coins Ike had found. If he had carried those when they searched him, there wouldn't be any chance in hell of her getting away. As it was, not finding any hint of the treasure, the three men eventually disappeared into the woods near the camp. She heard hoofbeats as they left.

It was another hour before she summoned the courage to go into the camp.

Sennick had been tortured as efficiently and effectively as if an Apache had worked him over. David Garrison had been slashed to bloody ribbons before he died. Terrence was a still smoldering lump of once human flesh. Cara and Irene lay on their backs. Their clothing had been ripped away. She didn't need to check to know they had been raped before having their throats slashed.

And then there was her husband.

Mirabelle dropped beside Ike and cried until no more

tears would flow. Replacing the grief was something Mira-belle didn't like, hardly recognized.

She wanted revenge and nothing would stop her from exacting it from the men who had gunned down her husband and committed such atrocities on the other five.

2

"That's one thing I like about you, Slocum. You don't drink when you're working." Jim "Beefsteak" Malone laughed his full-belly laugh and returned to industriously using a rag that might have cleaned off his boots before being applied to the shot glasses stacked in front of him. The rest of the back bar was in a similar slovenly condition, but it hardly mattered to the saloon's customers.

Slocum said nothing. The owner of the Damned Shame Drinking Emporium and Gambling Parlor never shut his piehole. That made him a good barkeep, but it irritated Slocum, who preferred his own company. Still, Beefsteak Malone had given him a job when he needed it most. There hadn't been a poker game in all of Sacramento that had gone his way. Some of the tinhorn gamblers were cheating, but Slocum hadn't been able to turn the cards against them. And the honest games had proven even worse for his poke. How anyone could lose with four queens was a poser, but he had. It had been a low straight diamond flush, but it had been drawn against him all right and proper.

Changing his luck by riding east, intending to find

someplace in Nevada to hole up for the winter, hadn't worked for him either. His horse had started coughing up its guts, and he had finally been forced to shoot it not three miles outside Grizzly Flats. Having the town so close had been his only good luck, though the walk in carrying his gear had been a chore on the rocky road.

Malone had taken one look at the worn ebony handle on the Colt Navy slung in a cross-draw holster and had offered him a job as bouncer in his saloon. Having only a dollar and a dime in his pocket, Slocum had accepted. So far the chore hadn't been too onerous. The clientele in the Damned Shame proved mostly peaceful, even when they got a snootful of Beefsteak's poisonous trade whiskey. He had broken up a couple fights, but the participants had been halfhearted, as if they wanted him to shove them apart, then escort them into the street, where they circled each other for a few minutes, then ended up staggering off to find another watering hole. From what Slocum could tell, saloons were Grizzly Flats' only real bright speck of prosperity. There were a dozen, and all seemed to turn a profit.

"I had one bouncer," Malone went on, "who claimed to never touch the stuff. Only when I found out that he was drunk all the time did I realize he meant water. Sober, the man was one mean son of a buck. Drunk, you couldn't tell. 'Cept for the smell."

"What's their story?" Slocum leaned back on the rough-hewn bar, both elbows supporting him as he stared across the room at the only pool table with green felt left on it. The other two had been so badly cut and scarred, any potential pool player would be better off using a barrel stave on rocks out in the muddy main street.

"Prospectors," Malone said scornfully. "Used to be a whale of a lot of gold around here, but that was nigh on twenty years back. Some folks never give up, though."

"Partners?"

"What else? An old married couple couldn't argue that

hard and not kill each other." Beefsteak drifted to the other end of the bar to tend a customer.

Slocum glanced at the saloon owner and decided the Damned Shame must be misnamed. Malone wore a head-light diamond just above his canvas apron, spent a tad too much time chowing down, and wore clothes more fitting for a bank president than a barkeep. He wore his hair slicked back and held down with a dollop of grease, making his head look like a round pumpkin. Slocum laughed ruefully. Even that description wasn't too far off. He had a sickly orange pallor that bespoke the long hours behind the bar and too little time out in the fresh air and bright sunlight.

"I'll rip yer guts out and strangle you with 'em!"

Slocum's attention snapped back to the two prospectors at the pool table. One waved around a crooked pool cue while the other gripped a seven ball as if he intended to cram it down his partner's throat. Slocum glanced over at Malone, who pointedly ignored the ruckus. Heaving a sigh, Slocum shoved away from the bar and walked slowly to the pool table.

"You gents playing or you intend to let somebody else in here?"

"You? You want to play some billiards?"

"Can't say that it's me wanting to play. We got a house full of boys interested, though."

The two forgot their argument and united against Slocum. He kept from laughing as they stepped shoulder to shoulder to confront their new common enemy. Both were close to knee-walking drunk and presented no real danger, except to each other.

"We . . . we got a game to play."

"Then I say, I'll put up a dollar to the winner." Slocum fished a greenback from his pocket and laid it on the corner of the table near a pocket.

"Winner take all!"

Slocum wasn't even sure which of the men spoke, but

both argued a mite over who would break, then started a game that didn't have much in the way of rules. He didn't care. They were playing peaceably enough and not causing any more trouble. He went back to the bar.

"Sure you don't want a snort, Slocum?" Beefsteak held up a bottle of Billy Taylor's Finest. "That was real purty the way you gentled those broncos."

"More buck and spin than bite. Keep your liquor and give me a dollar."

"Nope, that was yer doin'. Not part of the job description."

"Keeping the peace within these four walls is what you wanted me for."

Slocum couldn't complain too much. Despite his modest wages, he'd been able to buy a new horse and still had a few dollars in his pocket. Malone let him feed off whatever was left after the lunch trade disappeared. Unlike his name, the saloon owner didn't think much of real beef, preferring to serve his customers pickled eggs and occasional bits of fried chicken. Slocum thought the chickens were those that had stopped furnishing the rest of the luncheon menu, but he didn't ask. A piece of fried chicken now and again went down good, and he wasn't above drinking a beer with it.

But not when he worked. He wanted to keep a clear head.

He gritted his teeth when the doors slammed back and a bantam rooster of a man with a five-pointed star badge pinned on his vest stormed in. Marshal Willingham's attitude was twice the size of his body and a dozen times his brain capacity. That didn't stop him from throwing his weight around, ordering people to do his bidding. Slocum didn't see too many in Grizzly Flats jumping to obey, but he did see the seething rage etched like stone on the marshal's florid face.

He doubted the lawman was ever happy about anything. But then, Slocum wasn't sure he had anything to be happy about.

"Gimme a drink, Beefsteak," the lawman called out as he walked to the far end of the bar with a slightly bowlegged gait.

The saloon owner poured a drink and slid it over, then bent close and whispered to the marshal. The lawman got even angrier, his face turning bright red like a stewed tomato. Slocum reached over and slid the leather thong off his six-shooter's hammer. Men that mad threw down without thought and let lead fly all around. As crowded as the Damned Shame was, even if Willingham was a bad shot, people might die.

Truth was, Slocum wasn't averse to putting the marshal out of everyone's misery. Most folks in Grizzly Flats were friendly enough. The only one giving him grief wore that shiny star on his chest. Before he got his job as bouncer, Willingham had tried to run him out of town as an undesirable.

Slocum wondered if anyone in Grizzly Flats could be counted as desirable. Without much to keep the people in business, the honest ones would have moved on. Those left either sold whiskey, peddled human flesh, or worked to swindle their fellow citizens.

But he had seen worse places. If he worked through the winter, he would have more than enough to ride on to Middle Park in Colorado and find himself a job as a wrangler there for the summer.

Malone leaned away as the marshal glared at him. With a quick toss, Willingham knocked back the whiskey, spun, and stalked out. The barkeep made his way down the bar, making sure each of the customers had paid up and offering more liquor to those running dry. Not a one turned him down. By the time he reached Slocum, he had emptied another half bottle.

"Good night," Malone said.

"What'd he want? He looked mighty pissed."

"The marshal?" Malone made a dismissive gesture. "He's always fired up about something."

Slocum waited for the garrulous man to keep talking, but he didn't. That sparked Slocum's curiosity. He knew that saloon owners and the law in most towns had a cozy relationship. The marshal looked the other way if anything illegal went on, but Slocum hadn't seen anything like that in the Damned Shame. Beefsteak didn't even allow women into his establishment. This usually caused the law to demand a city license or some other fee—all meaning a bribe to turn a blind eye to the hookers. It was a cost of doing business, but Malone avoided that. From what Slocum could tell, Beefsteak had some sort of an agreement with a cathouse down the street. Any liquored-up customers wanting female companionship were escorted down there, but Slocum had never been told to do so.

That suited him just fine. He wasn't a pimp, and such an arrangement invited robbing the customers. For all the time he'd been in Grizzly Flats, he hadn't wandered down to that part of town to the south, where cathouses lined the streets.

"Hey, Slocum, want to play a hand or two of poker?"

He looked over his shoulder. Two regulars sat at a table with beer stains more prominent than the wood grain, a deck of cards between them. He had been in Grizzly Flats long enough to become a known commodity to the patrons, if not the cyprians.

He looked at Beefsteak, who shrugged.

"Do as you like. Your money. If you want to lose your money to those yahoos, that's your business. Just keep an eye out for trouble."

Slocum had a couple dollars left and had watched these two over the past week. They were what passed for top card players in Grizzly Flats. And he knew he was better.

He went to the table, hooked a toe around a chair rung, and pulled it out so he could sit.

"Penny ante? That's all I have."

"We'll take your money, no matter how little you have," said one, pushing back his hat to show a weathered forehead.

Above the hat band was nothing but pallid white skin. The man rode in the sun and weather and never took off the hat.

The other began shuffling, then passed the deck to Slocum to cut.

They began playing. Slocum let them win a few nickels to get a sense of how they played. He had pegged them right. They worked as a team, probably splitting their winnings. While they didn't cheat outright, one would fold rather than bluff if it looked as if his partner had a better hand. Slocum took this in stride and slowly began adding to the pile of coins in front of him. He had started with almost two dollars and won three off the men when the saloon doors slammed hard and a tough customer shoved his way in.

The man shook all over, getting water off his duster. He looked around, then fixed his gaze on Malone.

Slocum said, "Excuse me, gents. I've got to get to work." He scooped up the coins and dropped them into his coat pocket. As he stood, he was glad he had removed the keeper off his Colt's hammer earlier. It saved him from having to make such an overt move now.

"You get your ass out of here," Beefsteak called to the man. The owner cast a quick look over his shoulder at Slocum, who could not decipher the expression. It was a mixture of anger and fear.

Something more there bothered Slocum, as if Beefsteak Malone and the man were not exactly at odds with each other.

"I want it. I know you got it."

"Like hell. Get out. We'll talk about this later."

"Now, Beefsteak, we talk about this now." The man rested his hand on the butt of his six-gun.

Slocum walked forward slowly, not hurrying to spook the man but not slowing either. He stopped at the end of the bar, interposing himself between Beefsteak and the cantankerous gunman. The way he carried his shooting iron, the way he moved, how he watched Malone, all told Slocum this was a man who had no qualms about shooting down an opponent.

"Not seen you around town," Slocum said. "You new to Grizzly Flats?"

"Git outta my way," the man said. "This ain't none of your business."

"Slocum, he—" Malone started. He never got another word out.

The gunman went for his six-shooter. Slocum was faster. He stepped up and grasped the man's brawny wrist, preventing him from drawing. The man grunted as Slocum applied more pressure. Bones began grinding in the trapped wrist as Slocum tightened down even more.

When the gunman realized he wasn't going to outpower Slocum, he half turned and tried to knee his attacker in the groin. Slocum shifted his weight slightly, caught the knee on his outer thigh. He applied even more pressure on the man's wrist. This brought a cry of pain to the man's lips.

"Get out. I'd hate to bust your arm, but I will." There was no threat in Slocum's words, just promise.

"All right, all right." The man pushed Slocum back with his left hand. Slocum held on just long enough to let him know this wasn't the reason he was relaxing his grip.

Slocum stepped back, hands at his sides, elbows slightly bent. He could clear leather before the man got circulation back into his gun hand—and both of them knew it.

"This ain't over," the man said.

Slocum wasn't sure who he was talking to, him or Beefsteak. It didn't matter. The man backed away, still rubbing his right wrist, spun, and went back out into the freezing rain.

"Goddamn, Slocum, you didn't have to do that. He didn't mean no harm."

Slocum looked at the saloon owner and started to ask who he had just tossed into the storm. Beefsteak turned and rushed to the far end of the bar to keep from answering.

Whoever the gunman was, Malone knew him and they had a history. The barkeep wasn't afraid of him, but he should have been. Slocum had seen enough gunfights to know when a man was ready to draw. The one he had thrown out of the Damned Shame had been a hair away from sending a slug or two into Malone's guts.

Everyone in the saloon had fallen silent. Now they began whispering, eyes darting toward Slocum and then away if he tried to look directly at them. This would be talked about for days to come. Life was pretty dull in Grizzly Flats.

Beefsteak made a point of ignoring him, too, making Slocum even more curious. He touched his Colt Navy, then went to the swinging doors and looked out into the rain. White chunks of sleet mixed with the rain, preventing him from seeing as far as across the broad main street that meandered through the middle of town.

Slocum stepped out and knew instantly he was exposed to more than a late autumn storm. He heard boots scraping on the boardwalk to his right. Without hesitation, he half turned, hand flashing to the butt of his six-shooter. He drew, aimed, and fired just as the gunman cleared leather. Slocum's slug ripped through the man's belly, doubling him over. He staggered, went to one knee, and tried to raise his pistol. Slocum fired again.

The reports came as one. The man's round went wide of Slocum's head and was swallowed in the rain. Slocum's cut through the brim of the man's hat and plowed into his forehead. He toppled over. The .36-caliber bullet hadn't gone all the way through the man's head. Slocum knew it had rattled around, bouncing off skull bones and scrambling brains.

His thumb went to the hammer to draw it back again when Malone came running out, a sawed-off shotgun in his hands. Slocum noticed the man's composure. He wasn't shaken up by the shooting, and his quick glance at the corpse on the boardwalk in front of his saloon showed less fear than irritation.

"You had to push him, didn't you, Slocum?"

"He was waiting for me. I didn't have a choice."

"No, reckon not." Malone took a deep breath. His barrel chest expanded and light from the gas lamps just inside the saloon reflected off his diamond stickpin. He lowered the shotgun, sucked on his gums, then said, "You get rid of the body."

Before Slocum could ask what Beefsteak meant by that—dump the gunman in a gully and let the rain wash him away or find the town's undertaker—Marshal Willingham came running up. Behind him trailed a deputy and a few bedraggled townspeople coming to see what the commotion was about.

"What happened?" the red-faced marshal demanded. He looked from Slocum to Beefsteak, as if whatever had happened was the saloon owner's fault.

"Will," Beefsteak said, "come on inside and we'll talk it over. I told Slocum here to get rid of the body."

"That highwayman O'Dell is on the way, I know it. Who's gonna pay for the burial? Ain't the town. We ain't got money for a proper burial."

"The potter's field is good enough for the likes of him," Malone said. He put his arm around the marshal's shoulders and steered him inside.

Again Slocum wondered at the two. They weren't friends, not exactly, but they were more than adversaries. He looked at the dead body, already accumulating an icy sheen on the legs thrust out into the sleet.

"Let me through, let me through," a high-pitched voice demanded. A toothpick-slender man dressed in a black cloth cutaway coat and floppy-brimmed hat came up, pushing a wheelbarrow through the mud.

He lowered the handles and went to kneel beside the body. Quick fingers worked through the dead man's pockets, turning out a few damp greenbacks, a gold watch, and nothing else.

"You O'Dell?" Slocum asked.

"Yes, I am. I'm the town undertaker, sir." He made no move to hide the loot he had taken from the corpse. Slocum figured the undertaker was used to such robbery and probably considered it his due. If the marshal was right, this might be the undertaker's only pay for the funeral.

"Need help getting him into your wheelbarrow?"

"That would be appreciated, especially since you seem to be the one who caused this man's sad condition."

Slocum grunted as he got his arms around the gunman's body and heaved him upright. O'Dell moved the wheelbarrow forward as Slocum released his grip. The body fell neatly into the barrow. Without a word, O'Dell lifted the handles and pushed his way through the rain.

Slocum watched him vanish in the storm with his burden. As he started back into the saloon, movement caught his eye. He turned as the sheets of rain parted. He saw a woman standing in the downpour, arms around herself and shivering. The way she looked at him made a lump form in his throat. Before Slocum could say a word, she stepped away and disappeared into the storm as if she had never existed.

3

"Closing time, Slocum. Git on outta here," Beefsteak Malone said, throwing his grimy rag onto the bar and beginning to pull his apron off from his bulging gut. "Been a hell of a night." He laughed but without his usual boisterousness.

"Is the marshal giving you any trouble over the shooting?" Slocum watched his boss closely. A flicker of resentment crossed Malone's face, but he hid it quickly. By the time he came around the bar, there wasn't a trace of umbrage remaining.

"Don't worry yourself none over Will," he said. "He gets a bee in his bonnet now and then, but who cares about . . . a drifter?"

Slocum wondered why Malone checked what he was going to say. It didn't matter that much. Every town had its secrets, and this isolated, has-been town was no exception. He was the drifter, coming in with his saddle slung over his shoulder and down to his last dollar. He owed the saloon owner for giving him a job, especially one out of the foul weather.

He turned up his collar as he stepped into the storm. If

anything, it had grown worse. The wind drove the sleet at an angle, sneaking up under his hat brim. Slocum tugged it down and slogged through the muddy street, heading for the hotel a few doors down.

"See you tomorrow, Slocum. Don't be late!"

"Won't," Slocum called back. "I wouldn't miss that spread you put out at noon for anything."

Malone laughed as he made his way into the storm. He knew Slocum's sarcasm meant nothing. Free food was one small benefit of working in the saloon.

Slocum crossed the street and used the boot scraper outside the hotel's front door to get as much mud off as he could. He opened and closed the door as fast as he could to keep the heat in the hotel lobby from escaping into the freezing night.

"Evening, Mr. Slocum," the sleepy clerk said, throwing him a sloppy salute. For some reason the man thought of himself as a soldier, and Slocum was his superior. Slocum had been a captain in the CSA but wanted nothing more than to forget his service and the war.

He had been gut-shot by Bloody Bill Anderson for protesting Quantrill's raid on Lawrence, Kansas, and cutting down every male over the age of eight. Quantrill had been on a mission of revenge for slaughtered prisoners, including his own brother, but that hadn't been an excuse for killing children. Slocum had complained and been left for dead with a bullet where it caused the most pain and promised a slow death.

Slocum was tougher than even the hardened men in Quantrill's Raiders and had survived. By the time he recuperated, Quantrill was dead and he had no way of tracking down Bill Anderson. He had returned to Slocum's Stand in Georgia, his parents dead and his brother, Robert, killed during Pickett's Charge on the last day of the Battle of Gettysburg. All he had wanted was to find peace. Instead he found a carpetbagger judge who had taken a fancy to the farm. The Reconstruction judge probably thought it would be easy to force a debilitated man like a wounded veteran off his property with a bogus unpaid tax lien.

In one respect, the judge had been right. Slocum didn't stay on the farm. And the judge did. In a grave. Next to the gunman he had ridden out with to seize the farm. Slocum had ridden west and never again considered becoming a farmer, preferring to live by his wits and quick gun. Wanted posters for federal judge killing dogged his steps, but if he kept moving, he stayed ahead of the law.

He nodded in the night clerk's direction. This was good enough for the young lad to smile broadly, showing a broken front tooth.

Slocum trudged up the steps to the second story, turned at the landing, and went up to the third floor. Every stair was increasingly rickety so he watched how he stepped. Halfway up to the third floor and his room, he paused and looked at the stairs. Then he looked up ahead and slipped his pistol from its holster. He wished he had reloaded, but only a round or two would be adequate.

He reached the top floor, which should have been empty. The damp spots on the stairs and the floor leading to his room warned him someone had preceded him. Stopping in front of the door, he carefully turned the ceramic doorknob, then shoved the door open. His six-shooter came up and centered on the dark figure sitting on the side of his bed.

"I'm not armed," came a tiny voice. "I saw you kill him."

Slocum stepped into the room and kicked the door shut with his boot heel. He was slower to holster his six-shooter. He fumbled in his vest pocket, found his tin of lucifers, and lit a coal oil lamp on the table holding a small washbasin and pitcher. The resulting soft yellow light after he trimmed the wick bathed his unexpected guest.

It was the woman he had momentarily seen standing in the storm earlier. She looked like a drowned rat. Her brown hair hung in wet strands. Her dress had seen better days, being torn as well as wet and plastered against her thin body. Slocum doubted she had been eating regularly from the way her cheeks were sunken, and her eyes had a dark, haunted look about them.

"Do you always break into strangers' rooms?"

"I didn't have anywhere else to go. I don't have much." She reached down and ran her finger around something in her dress pocket. Slocum couldn't tell what it was but it was small and round and not a hideout gun.

Somehow, he didn't think he had anything to fear from her. If she had been the dead gunman's lady out for revenge, she would have shot him down from ambush. Even if she had wanted to watch him crawl, have him apologize, somehow make amends for the two bullets in the gunman's body, back shooting him was an easier road to travel. After all, she had to know how good he was with his six-shooter.

"Let's start over," Slocum said, perching against the washstand. His body ached and he wanted nothing more than to stretch out on the bed to get some sleep, but he felt that making her move might spook her. For some reason, he wanted to find out what her story might be.

"I saw you kill him. If you hadn't, I would have. I would have tried," she amended. From the set to her jaw and the way she shook all over—and not from the cold—Slocum believed her.

"Who was he?"

"I don't know."

Slocum thought he was past being surprised about anything that happened around him. He was wrong.

"You don't know who he was but you'd've killed him yourself? I don't even know why he tried to gun me down."

"Pure cussedness," she said with a bitterness that put him on guard. "He killed my husband. Him and two other men. Or maybe there was more of 'em. Can't rightly say."

"Robbery?"

"Something like that."

"He was crazy as a bedbug. He killed your husband and stole what you owned?"

"Him and others murdered my friends and Ike."

Slocum said nothing. She worked up the courage to keep talking, and he wasn't sure why. Something had brought her to his room, but if the man responsible for murdering her husband was dead, what she thought to get from him was a poser.

"You have a name?"

"Mirabelle," she said. "Mirabelle Comstock." She almost choked on the name. Slocum introduced himself and then fell silent again.

More often than not, folks spoke to fill a void. For his part, Slocum preferred silence. That was one reason he enjoyed traveling from one place to another alone, out on the range or in the mountains with only his horse and the wind as companions. Needless chatter bored him.

"There was at least three of them. I want you to find the other two that I know of."

"I'm not a killer for hire. That owlhoot forced my hand tonight. Otherwise, I would never have paid him a second glance."

"Then find who the other two are and I'll do the chore."

"This isn't my fight. Tell the marshal."

"He's not reliable. I asked 'fore I came to you. Nobody in Grizzly Flats thinks much of Marshal Willingham."

"Can't say I'd disagree either. Then find the sheriff and tell him."

"I don't have any way of getting out of Grizzly Flats. I . . . I'm stuck here. Besides, where would I go? Ike was all the family I had. Him and the others were my friends." Mirabelle looked off into the distance, focused on something beyond the wall with its peeling wallpaper. "They were Ike's friends, but I got along all right with Cara."

"Were you moving here? Or were you on your way to somewhere else to homestead?" The way her attention snapped back to him made Slocum wonder what the men and women had been up to.

"I can pay you."

"You said you were flat busted, that the road agents stole everything you had."

"They destroyed most of our gear. They didn't even bother taking it. They raped Cara and Irene. Tortured and murdered the men. Hell, I don't know. They might have raped them, too. They was animals what they did."

"So how can you pay me if I was fool enough to agree?"

She ran her fingers around the small hard circles pressed into her dress pocket. She reared back, fumbled a mite, then pulled out two gold coins. Even in the weak light from the oil lamp the twenty-dollar gold pieces shone with an inner radiance that caught Slocum's full attention.

"That's enough to get you to San Francisco or Virginia City or about anywhere you'd want to go. You could live for a couple weeks, catch a stagecoach, and still have one of those twenty-dollar pieces left to help you along."

She held out her palm. The two coins beckoned to Slocum. He took them, ran his thumbnail around the edge, and didn't find any milling. Holding one coin close to the lamp let him examine it. The disk was worn smooth, erasing any hint of the coin's origin. He bit down on the edge. His tooth sank into the soft metal, telling him this was gold.

"Might be lead," he said to her. He held the coin closer to the light. Where his tooth had scored the coin showed nothing but more gold.

"It's real, isn't it?" She smiled at the question. They both knew the answer.

"I can't take all you own. If it's as you said—"

"It is!"

"—then you ought to think of this as your husband's legacy to you. Take it and forget revenge."

"I can't forget. You didn't see what them animals did.

No, they was worse than animals. A beast would only kill. They tortured and then mutilated and killed."

He tucked the two coins into his vest pocket next to his brother's watch. That seemed appropriate. The coins were Mirabelle's inheritance from her husband. The watch was all Robert had left him after being killed at Gettysburg.

"I don't know where to start. How will you find them?" Mirabelle asked.

Slocum tapped the watch pocket as a thought came to him.

"Pickett's Charge," he said softly.

"What?"

"Picket's Charge . . . Gettysburg . . . the attack on Cemetery Ridge . . . the cemetery."

"I don't understand," she said.

"The undertaker took the man I killed tonight. He'll bury him tomorrow. Might be interesting to see who shows up for the funeral."

"His partners," Mirabelle said, her eyes glowing with excitement. "I knew I'd done the right thing coming to you, Mr. Slocum."

Slocum hesitated then, not knowing what to do. He finally moved around the bed to the opposite side, sat, and kicked off his boots. By the time he had his gun belt off and hanging on the brass post, Mirabelle had shifted around and sat with her hands in her lap, staring at him with her wide brown eyes.

"You can go or stay. Doesn't matter."

"I don't have anywhere to go."

"I snore," Slocum said, stretching out. He rolled onto his side, his back to her. It took a few minutes but the bed finally sagged as Mirabelle stretched out.

Before Slocum fell asleep, her arm draped over him, he heard her sob quietly and then finally begin to snore louder than he ever could. Wondering what he was getting himself into, he finally drifted off to sleep.

* * *

Slocum came awake with a start when he felt cold, wet air on his face. He had his Colt Navy half out of its holster before he realized Mirabelle had opened the tiny window and stood staring out. From the pale light silhouetting her, it was just barely sunrise.

He yawned, stretched, and sat up. She turned to him.

"When is the funeral?" she asked.

"Can't imagine the undertaker—O'Dell's his name—will be in any hurry to plant the body."

"I . . . I want to come with you. I didn't see the others all that good. It was dark, but I think I'd know them."

Slocum understood. Sometimes going with a feeling in the gut proved better than waiting for hard evidence. Mirabelle might be able to identify the men just by their attitude, the way they walked, or the set of their bodies, even if she hadn't seen their faces.

Then a worry came to him.

"They see your face?"

"No, no, I was hid. Ike rushed in and got himself killed, but he protected me. They don't even know anyone escaped."

Slocum wondered if that was right but didn't press the matter. Any of the killers who showed up at their partner's funeral and recognized Mirabelle would give themselves away. That was risky, but Slocum felt sure he could handle any no-accounts who would slaughter men and rape women as those did.

"Let's make our way out to the cemetery. You know where it is?" Slocum asked.

"We never came to town. Leastwise, not me. Lucas Sennick came in and got drunk, but he's dead and—"

"All right," Slocum interrupted, seeing that Mirabelle was starting off on a wild tangent. From the set to her shoulders, she was ready to break. "Might be better if you stayed here and let me go."

"I want to," she said, but Slocum saw how she hunted for a plausible way out. She wanted to bring the outlaws to justice—at the end of a rope or maybe in front of a six-shooter she held—but her courage was fading fast.

"I only have my horse," he said. "We'd draw attention if we rode up together on it," he said. It sounded lame but gave her an excuse. She nodded.

As he pulled on his boots, she came to him and reached out timidly. Her hand shook as she touched his shoulder.

"Thank you."

"Being paid for it," he said, touching his vest pocket. He stood, strapped on his gun belt, and finally shrugged into his coat. It surprised him when Mirabelle helped settle it down so it wasn't wrinkled.

He looked at her. The fear was receding but her doe eyes made her appear especially vulnerable.

He left the room without another word. It took fifteen minutes to get to the livery stables, get directions, and saddle up. He rode slowly along the road. Keeping to the shoulder proved easiest since the mud and ice mix in the deep ruts would slow his horse. He didn't want the icy shards to cut his horse's legs. Keeping away from the worst potholes let him crunch through unsullied ice.

Slocum reached the cemetery by following the signs. They were freshly painted and each carried a small advertisement for O'Dell's Funeral Parlour. Slocum wondered if the cadaverous undertaker had any competition or if this was simply his way of feeling important, seeing his name on every signpost on the way to the town cemetery.

The burial ground had a low stone wall running parallel to the road. A cast iron arch had begun to rust, but once under it, the rows of graves were well kept. Some had headstones and even the ones marked with wooden crosses were maintained. Whether this was something O'Dell did, too, Slocum couldn't tell.

At the back of the cemetery, O'Dell stood supervising two men hauling a pine coffin from the back of a wagon. Slocum dismounted, tethered his horse on a wooden cross, then walked slowly toward where an open grave yawned. He looked around. Other than the undertaker and his two assistants, no one else had shown up for the burial.

"Come to pay your respects, Slocum?" O'Dell spoke slowly and his voice had lowered to a rumbling bass appropriate for mourning.

"Seemed like the decent thing to do since I was the one who put him in the ground."

"Well, yes," O'Dell said, his professional sorrow momentarily disturbed.

"That his marker?" Slocum pointed to a flat stone in the wagon.

"It is. I need to get the stonemason to chip in the name and date but thought it fitting to lay him to rest and take care of such details later."

"Cost a pretty penny," Slocum said.

"It isn't *that* expensive."

"Who paid for it?"

"I . . . I don't know. I found an envelope with adequate money thrust under my door with instructions."

"You ever get his name?"

"I have, sir," O'Dell said stiffly. "That was information included with the money. Mr. Rupert Eckerly."

The name meant nothing to Slocum. From the way the undertaker spoke, it meant nothing to him either.

"You have anything to say over the grave, Mr. Slocum?"

"Get on with it," Slocum said. He watched the two assistants lower the coffin into the grave.

O'Dell reached into his pocket and took out a Bible, thumbed it to a page, and began reading sonorously. Slocum considered taking off his hat, then decided not to since that would be hypocritical. When he had cut down Eckerly, he had only been defending himself. It wasn't until later that Mirabelle Comstock had indicted the man in brutal killing and rape.

As O'Dell read on, Slocum turned slowly and looked across the cemetery to the rusty arch. A man sat astride a horse there, a bandanna pulled up over his face. Chilly wind blew off the mountains and across the cemetery, but the cloth wouldn't do much to protect the man's face. Slocum decided he wasn't interested in being identified.

As O'Dell rambled on, Slocum turned and walked back to his horse. The undertaker sped up to conclude the ceremony now that he had lost his only audience. Swinging into the saddle, Slocum rode toward the road.

The other onlooker had already hightailed it.

Slocum wondered if the man would have come to the graveside if he hadn't been there. Finding out would go a way toward answering questions that piled up.

The muddy road didn't hold tracks well, but the rider had cut across the road and plowed through open field. One set of tracks came toward the cemetery, another went away. Slocum didn't have to be much of a tracker to know where the man had come from and where he returned. He put his heels to his horse's flanks and trotted across the snowy terrain.

The man had made a hasty retreat, daring to gallop his horse where Slocum felt secure only in a trot over the hidden, frozen land. But there was no hiding the trail as it meandered up through the foothills toward a canyon angling away sharply.

The tracks led deeper into the canyon. Slocum slowed his advance and looked around. The stillness came from the snow damping the sound. Slocum played on this to keep after the fleeing rider without fear of being overheard.

As he followed the trail close to boulders, he stopped. The tracks changed. He didn't dismount as he deciphered their message. The rider had halted, wheeled his horse around, and then continued along the trail.

Slocum stiffened. The rider knew he was being trailed. He must have spotted—

Before Slocum could finish his thought, a rock crashed down on his head, knocking him from his horse.

4

Slocum struggled in the snow and mud, trying to get to his feet. He hit a slippery patch and fell facedown. The shock of icy water against his nose and mouth brought him fully alert. His head throbbed from the rock that had bounced off his crown, but his hat had robbed the missile of some power. That didn't make his situation any less perilous.

He rolled to the side as another rock crashed down from the top of the boulder he had passed. Standing atop the huge rock was a masked man—not the one he had followed.

When the man saw he wasn't getting anywhere with his rain of rocks, he went for his six-shooter. Slocum kicked hard, skidded along the ground, and slid on his back. He reached for his own six-gun, but the metallic sound of a hammer cocking froze him faster than the icy ground ever could.

"You're a dead man if you draw that hogleg," came a muffled voice.

Slocum craned around and saw another masked man sighting down the twin barrels of a shotgun. He slowly thrust out his hands—without filling either with the butt of his Colt.

"What's going on? You road agents?"

"Shut up!" the man atop the rock called down. Slocum turned his attention upward, something gnawing at the edge of his brain. Then he blacked out entirely when the shotgun-toting outlaw clobbered him on the side of the head with a hard, cold metallic barrel.

When he was again aware of pain, he forced himself to keep his eyes shut. Let them think he was still knocked out. But something betrayed him. His eyelids might have fluttered or he could have moaned. Slocum wasn't sure what it was, but a hard blow to his jaw snapped his head to the side.

"Why you followin' me?"

Slocum winced as new pain assaulted him. The man used his pistol to beat him. The barrel smacked into his temple. Bone didn't break but blazing white stars danced about. Then the man used the butt on his chin again. Slocum was quickly reaching the point where he wouldn't be able to speak, even if he wanted to. He felt his lips swelling from the blows, and the ringing in his head made hearing something of a chore.

He squinted to try to focus his eyes. Four men stood in a half circle around him. All wore heavy tan canvas dusters, hats pulled low almost to their eyes and bandannas up over their noses. Trying to figure out how tall they were didn't work. There wasn't anything to judge height by. All he could do was say one was taller or shorter than the road agent standing beside him.

"Shoot him and let's get outta here."

"Tell me!" The pistol swung, and Slocum sensed rather than saw it coming. He jerked hard at the last possible instant, robbing the barrel of its power. He flung himself across the trail and halfway over the edge of the embankment. Below him lay the canyon bottom with a river partially frozen over. That was clearer than his images of the outlaws.

He grunted as a boot crashed into his ribs.

"We got to get outta here. Kill him, will you? Or I will."

They argued over whether to keep questioning Slocum or kill him outright. From the pain lancing into his ribs and through his head, he wasn't sure which he preferred. He half rose up. He grunted as the boot came swinging for his belly, but he didn't let it connect. He grabbed the foot and twisted, using his weight more than his strength to throw the outlaw off balance.

They crashed down together. Slocum was ready, if injured, and swarmed up to grab the man's wrist. He forced the gun away from him. Anger erased his pain for a moment; the owlhoot used Slocum's own gun to pistol-whip him.

Fingers wrapping around the ebony butt, he tried to turn the muzzle around so he could end the son of a bitch's life.

He heard the report, but it took a second to realize that he hadn't fired. Another of the outlaws had. The warmth of blood spread on his side. Then pain blotted out the world. Slocum half rose, then toppled over, rolling down the embankment to the river's frozen banks. Water splashed against his face, as excruciating as the pulsing pain in his ribs and the strange tingling in his legs.

Fiercely gripping his six-shooter, he tried to roll over to get a shot at the men above him along the trail. Nothing worked. Arms refused to move. His legs felt like lead. His vision faded. He sank back, his cheek in the sluggishly flowing ice water.

He never quite passed out but couldn't move. Listening to the water rippling past, the sound of birds high above, the occasional crack of ice breaking free to fall into the river, John Slocum focused on not feeling pain. Soon enough, the cold stole away the worst of the pain, but in a far-off corner of his brain, he realized he was freezing to death.

A moment's panic that he was going blind galvanized him to roll over and sit up, the six-gun still in his hand. His trigger finger was too numb to draw back, but there was no need. And he wasn't blind. The sun had dipped behind the canyon walls, plunging the riverbed into twilight.

The movement caused some pain but not as much as before. In a sitting position, he pulled back his coat, vest, and shirt. The bullet hadn't even penetrated his chest but had skipped along a rib. That didn't make it hurt any less, but not having to worry about lead poisoning buoyed his spirits.

He was going to live. He was going to put all four of the road agents in graves alongside Rupert Eckerly.

This thought fixed in his head, he got to his feet. It took several tries before he got his Colt holstered. Then he began the treacherous climb up the slope to the road. Loose rock made it difficult. His battered condition added to the time and effort it took, but he finally reached the trail where he had been ambushed. To his surprise, his horse stood nearby, waiting for him.

A wild thought raced through his mind that the road agents wanted him to step up so they could shoot him from the saddle. Then he realized he was a touch feverish, and it wasn't likely men such as those who had waylaid him would wait for him. They'd plug him from the road. Chances were good they thought he was dead.

He had to climb onto a rock and then flop across the saddle to mount. He took the reins and aimed the horse back along the trail toward distant Grizzly Flats.

The horse took him to the livery stable around midnight.

He came awake with a start. Something was wrong, very wrong. He reached for his six-gun but it wasn't at his left hip. He groped about and finally realized he wasn't even dressed. The darkness hid everything, but he was warm and not drowning in the icy river.

"Calm yourself, Mr. Slocum. Lie back."

"Where am I?"

"In your hotel room." Mirabelle's voice was soft and her breath warm in his ear as she whispered to him. "I can light the lamp, if you like."

"No need." Slocum lay back and tried to relax. His left side was stiff. He gently explored where he had been shot and found he had been bandaged.

"I patched you up best I could. That was a nasty scratch on your side."

"I was shot," he said. "But not good enough to kill me."

"You are truly a hard man to kill," she said.

He felt the bed sag as she sat. Her rump pressed into his thigh as she moved back so she wasn't hanging on the edge of the bed.

"Men have found that out," he said. *And died for the oversight,* he silently added. There'd be four more when he got his strength back.

"I got some broth into you. Are you thirsty?"

"I'm all right." He shivered under the covers.

"You were running a fever, but that went away a couple hours ago."

"What time is it?"

"Close to sunrise," Mirabelle said. "The stableman didn't know who to tell about you, so he came to the hotel, figuring the clerk might know. He said he'd've told somebody named Beefsteak but the saloon was closed."

"My boss. The owner of the Damned Shame," Slocum said.

"The two of us, the stableman and me, we got you up here. He gave me some clean bandages, too. I didn't put any of the horse liniment on since it was so vile smelling."

Slocum stretched and felt the bruises stiffening. He would have been better off if she had held her nose and applied the stinging liniment, but he said nothing. She had done the best she could, and he was alive.

He was alive and mad as hell.

"I saw a man at the funeral and followed him," Slocum said. "He ambushed me. Him and three others."

"Three? But the one you killed . . ."

"Could there have been five men at the massacre?"

"I only saw three, but I wasn't thinking straight. They might have had others strung out 'round the camp as sentries. Watchin' their horses? I just don't know!" Her voice turned shrill, and she came close to hysteria.

"Don't much matter if these gents were there or not," Slocum said. He tried to remember every detail about them but getting hit so hard had rattled him and knocked loose a few memories. He remembered dusters and hats and bandannas and not much else. "I might have shot one of them."

"Kill him?" The vitriol in Mirabelle's words sharpened his senses.

"Don't think so." He shivered.

"You're real cold. All the blankets in the room are piled on top of you."

Before he could say anything, the bed sagged again and he felt her stretch out beside him—under the covers. She snuggled closer, her body pressing warmly into his. Somehow, the bruises didn't seem to bother him quite so much. He moaned when her hand began moving over his muscular belly and then worked lower.

"This isn't hurting you none?"

"No," he said. And her hand gripped him, teasing his limpness until he was rigid and throbbing.

She began moving up and down, her hand stroking his length and sending tiny jabs of delight into his loins. He hardened even more as his heart pounded.

"That feels mighty fine."

"But it's not doing much to warm you. Not like this."

The covers tented up as she scooted down in the bed. Her hand was quickly replaced by her soft lips. She kissed the tip of his organ, then began licking from the head back down to his balls. Her tongue danced lightly over the tightening sac, causing him to squirm.

"Am I hurting you?" came her muffled voice.

"No, no, not at all," he got out. He shifted his hips around to better let her have free rein. He was immediately rewarded.

She took the plum tip into her mouth and used her tongue all over it. Then she slowly took more of him into her mouth. He felt the sensitive tip rub across her inner cheek as she cradled him with her rough tongue. Then she used her teeth to lightly score the sides. He rose off the bed in reaction. She backed away until only a small part of his manhood remained in her mouth until he sank back.

Then she began bobbing up and down, driving him deeper into her mouth and throat with every move. He gasped and reached down to lace his fingers through her hair. He found only the top of the coverlet. Trying to work his hands underneath the blankets proved harder than he'd expected. His mind wandered as she began sucking harder on him. Lewd sounds were barely muffled by the blankets as she avidly worked.

Pressures built within him. He tried to hold them back, but her insistent mouth wore away at his control.

"No, no, stop. I want to—"

He never got any farther. She began sucking just the tip of his cock, her tongue swirling across the sensitive underside as she fingered his balls. The gust of her hot breath against his flesh, coupled with the up and down motion of her head, was enough to rob him of any good intention to give as good as he was receiving.

His hips rose off the bed again as he tried to drive hard and fast into her face. She sucked every drop he spilled and then, too soon, he began to turn limp. Slocum sank back to the bed, drained emotionally and physically.

"I wanted to—"

"Later," she said, working her way up to lie close to him. She snaked her arm across his chest and pulled him closer in the narrow bed. Mirabelle might have been dressed but he felt her heaving body.

"I'll hold you to that," he said. Slocum found it harder to keep his eyes open. Sleep sneaked up on him. "I owe you."

"Sleep, Mr. Slocum, rest. You need to rest."

"All warm and relaxed now," he said. "And call me John."

"Good night . . . John."

He slept for ten hours before waking, ready to whip his weight in wildcats.

5

"Are you all right, John?" Mirabelle asked.

"Still stiff," he said, trying to twist and feeling a twinge where she had bandaged his ribs.

"Oh, really?" She looked at his crotch.

"Not there."

She laughed for the first time since he had met her, and he liked the sound.

"Can be," she said, her smile broadening.

"Later. I want to go over the campsite where your husband and the others were murdered." Slocum regretted saying that since the woman's smile melted like snow in the morning sun. The good mood had been crushed by the memory of the deaths, but Slocum wanted to study the area for clues as to how many killers had taken part in the murders and rapes before the weather wiped out all trace.

"It's a ways," she said, not looking at him now. She stared out across Grizzly Flats and to the edge of town. "I walked it before. Not sure I'm up to that again."

"I've got money enough to rent a buggy," he said, though not wanting to spend either of the two twenty-dollar gold pieces she'd paid him. Better to use what coins he had won in the poker game first. Slocum preferred riding, but the jostling in the saddle might hurt him too much. He was still on the mend and wanted to be in fighting shape when he ran those bastards to ground.

"I don't want to put you out. I can give you directions."

He knew she tried to find reasons not to torment herself with the site that had changed her life so drastically. Although he hated to force her, he needed her to go over every move and show him every spot where the killers had stood, how they had set up the attack, the direction they had taken when they left. Even if she gave him exact directions to the campsite, none of the other information so necessary to learning what the outlaws had done would be available to him without her showing him.

They rented the buggy from the stable owner for a dollar. Slocum hitched up his horse, helped Mirabelle into the buggy, then settled himself and snapped the reins. The horse preferred a rider on its back, and Slocum commiserated. This was necessary, as was torturing Mirabelle with the crime scene once more.

The trip along the muddy road passed in silence. For Slocum's part, he didn't need anything more than occasional stabs of Mirabelle's finger, pointing the proper route. Trying to remember everything about the attack that had laid him up proved futile. He'd as soon chew off his own leg than admit he couldn't identify the men he had promised to kill.

If he'd had only slight interest in bringing them to justice because of what they had done to Isaac Comstock and the others, it had sharpened after the men waylaid him. Although the gang ambushing him might be a different one from those who had killed the Comstock party, he doubted it. Rupert Eckerly was the bridge between the attacks. Mirabelle identified the dead man as one of her assailants. It would be too much of a coincidence if Eckerly had been part of two gangs.

"Up there," she said in a small voice. "We camped just

inside the mouth of that canyon. Spring Canyon, Terrence called it."

Slocum worked the buggy up the trail as close as he could to where Mirabelle had indicated the camp, but the slope was too great and the rocks too large to get closer than a hundred yards. He set the brake, made sure the horse was tethered and close to dry clumps of grass, then helped the woman to the camp.

The closer they got, the more Mirabelle shook. She cried openly when they came to the site of the massacre.

Slocum had seen savagery during the war—and had taken part in more than his share—but the bodies showed how brutal the outlaws' questioning had been.

Animals had dined on the corpses, but there was no mistaking how one man had been skinned. From what Mirabelle had heard that night, the torture had occurred to make the man talk. He didn't find enough left of the women's bodies but had no doubt they had been raped because of the way their clothing had been ripped. Coyotes wouldn't care. Indeed, some pieces had been carried off by scavengers. Arms and even legs were missing, but that didn't take away from how Slocum reconstructed the scene before him.

Coyotes were animals operating on a simple instinct to stay alive. The men responsible for the deaths were cold-blooded and calculating in their actions.

"Could any of them have known where the gold was hidden?"

"No, no," Mirabelle said in a choked voice. "I don't even know where Ike found those coins, but he thought they were part of the treasure."

"How'd you get the information this was the place to search?"

Slocum paced slowly around the site of the killings, trying to decipher what was left of the tracks. Animals had obliterated much of the spoor, and the rain and light snow had added to the problem of finding how many had attacked the camp. Once, he dropped to his knees and brushed away a drift of unsullied snow. He was rewarded with a pair of boot prints.

"Did you find anything, John?"

"Still looking," he said. "Who told you about the gold?"

"Somebody in Sacramento told Terrence. He hung out with lowlifes. I don't rightly know what Ike saw in him, but they was good friends."

"Ike knew him before he met you?" When there wasn't an answer, he turned to see Mirabelle fighting to keep from crying. He was at the end of getting answers about the source of the clues regarding the gold.

He usually scoffed at treasure maps, lost mines, and hidden gold because the men selling such information were swindlers out to make a quick dollar from the gullible. There were different ways of selling the worthless. Soapy Smith in Denver made a fortune selling bars of soap. A few confederates in the audience where he made his spiel unwrapped the soap he sold and found ten-dollar bills. Another would find a fifty. By the time Smith had sold crates of the cheap soap, he had gathered his partners and taken back the money he had used to "salt" the bars. Very few paying exorbitant prices for the bars found anything but lye soap.

Slocum had always thought they got what they deserved. Most of the men probably had never used a bar of soap in years. That was a harmless swindle. Selling maps to hidden mines in remote mountains put the trusting buyers in danger from Indians, starvation, and even bad weather. He had no idea what would have happened to Mirabelle's party if they had been caught in one of the early snows. From what she said, they had sent one of the party into Grizzly Flats to buy what supplies they could afford and ended up with damned little.

He left her sitting on a rock to one side of the camp and began a spiral search, slowly going farther from the center until he found where the killers had left their horses before attacking. The ground proved too muddy for him to find the number of horses, but the limbs of scrub oaks showed signs of bridles being secured. He counted twice, being sure he was right. Returning to camp, he caught Mirabelle dabbing at her eyes.

She looked up, her brown eyes wide and bloodshot.

"What did you find?"

"The men in camp didn't have a chance. There were five, maybe six who came in."

"I didn't see any but the three."

"Don't know where the other three were. My guess is they were up in the rocks to shoot down into camp, if the need arose. Terrence and the others were caught in a trap and didn't have a chance to escape. There wasn't a blamed thing they could have done."

Slocum wasn't sure he believed that. Terrence or whoever fancied himself to be in charge should have posted a sentry. That was common sense, no matter what the reason they were out here. He doubted Sennick would have agreed, and the other man in camp, Garrison, probably had his hands full doing two men's work. Terrence wouldn't have lowered himself to watch for intruders.

He shrugged off the lack of caution. No one out hunting for gold thought they were in danger. They hadn't found anything yet.

"Why'd they attack when they did?" he wondered aloud.

"What's that?" Mirabelle came over, her shoes making crunching sounds in the thin blanket of snow.

"The killers didn't come from Sacramento. Whoever told Terrence about the stolen gold wasn't going to follow, then attack before you found anything."

"But Ike thought he had!"

"He hadn't told anyone in camp. The owlhoots were here before you came back with the coins."

"I never thought of that. Maybe they didn't know we was hunting for gold. Maybe they was just outlaws."

Slocum knew that wasn't true. She had heard the killers demanding to know where the gold was.

"Tell me about Sennick." He continued rummaging through the debris left by the scavengers as Mirabelle related random observations about her onetime partner. Nothing hit him until she spoke of sending Sennick into town.

"He wouldn't do chores around the camp. Said that was women's work, but he wouldn't do any of the chores the men would either. Ike was always angry about him. That's why we sent him to town to get our supplies."

"And he got drunk," Slocum said, standing on a rock to get a better look around the camp. "Who do you think he'd tell about you hunting for the gold?"

"We swore him to secrecy," Mirabelle said, but her voice told the truth. She believed he had shot off his mouth and caused the killers to come hunting for the gold.

"He probably was so drunk, whoever he told thought you'd found the gold. Or maybe he was boasting. A lie about easy gold is as likely to be believed. Grizzly Flats isn't prosperous."

"The lure of gold would be too much," she said. "It surely was for us. Until Ike found them coins, I hardly believed there was anything out here."

Slocum jumped down and braced himself for what he had to say to her.

"It's not right leaving them out where the coyotes can finish dining on them," he said. "If you were hunting for gold, somebody must have a shovel."

"We all did." She walked as if her feet were stuck in water buckets, rummaged through a pile of material, and brought Slocum a shovel. "This was Ike's. Ours."

"The ground isn't frozen yet, and as muddy as it is, digging won't be too hard," he said. "Why don't you take what you need from the stores?" He wanted to keep her mind off the mass grave he intended to dig. Individual graves would take too long.

"All right, John, I'll do that." She took two steps and, still facing away from him, said, "Could you bury Ike separate from the others? He *was* my husband."

He silently began digging a large pit and moved the bodies of the two women and three men into it. From the way Mirabelle hovered over the corpse at the edge of camp, he knew that had to be Ike. His back and side ached horribly by the time he'd finished the chore. Digging was easy enough, but every shovelful was heavier than he'd expected since he lifted mud rather than just earth.

He carefully searched each body before filling in the dirt. The outlaws had been thorough, robbing everyone. Watches, rings, any money—all gone. Slocum tamped the final shovel worth of mud over the mass grave, then went to where Mirabelle sat on a rock, staring at her husband's corpse.

Slocum moved to cut off her view as he rolled the body over. Varmints had eaten away the man's face. He worked quickly to dig the grave but soon ran into rock. Rather than waste time finding another spot, he continued, moved Isaac Comstock into the two-foot-deep grave, and filled it back in. He did take the time to pile rocks on the grave. It wouldn't deter a hungry coyote but might slow the better-fed ones.

"You want to say words over his grave?"

Mirabelle stood beside him. She had tied two sticks together into a cross.

"He wasn't like that. When we got married, he didn't even want a minister. He found a judge to marry us." Mirabelle sniffed a little. "Ike paid him with a pint of whiskey. This will have to do." She shoved the cross into the soft dirt, then used rocks to prop it upright.

The first winter storm that blew down the canyon would steal away the marker. It might even open the grave, but Slocum doubted Mirabelle was going to make a pilgrimage back here once they left.

"The best thing to do is go back to Grizzly Flats and find who Sennick was spilling his drunken guts to," he said.

"I have a few things. My clothes, the ones that weren't too ripped up. Some other things. No call to take anything belonging to Ike. The killers done stole ever'thing off his body."

Slocum touched the coins in his pocket. If Ike hadn't given them to Mirabelle, the outlaws would have discovered them—and tortured him until he revealed the place where he'd found them.

She looked up at him, her expression neutral.

"I want to find the gold. Let's go into the canyon, and I'll show you where Ike found the coins."

Slocum started to point out they didn't have any supplies and would either have to go on foot or ride double on his horse. A small sound, hardly audible to anyone without his sharp senses, came from deeper in the canyon Mirabelle had indicated.

"You gather what you can for us," he said. "I want to take one more look around to be sure there were only five. Chances are there might have been one more than that."

"But you—" Mirabelle stared at him when she realized he wanted her to be a decoy while he scouted. "All right, John, I'll do that." Her words carried since she spoke louder than necessary. She reached out and gripped his arm, then released him and began moving about the camp aimlessly.

Slocum wished he had his rifle, but he had left it with his saddle and other gear in town. Moving like a ghost, he went to a tower of rocks overlooking the camp. This was where Terrence should have posted a lookout.

Making his way up the rock, finding footholds and ripping his fingers on the sharp edges, he finally reached the summit. Keeping flat on his belly, he slithered around. He stopped when he looked down. Not six inches from his nose was a shiny spent brass cartridge. At least one of the killers had been posted here and had fired into the unsuspecting treasure hunters below.

Slocum chanced a look over the edge. It was an easy shot.

He had been a sniper during the war and could have shot everyone below before they knew there was a problem. Craning his neck a mite put strain on his injured rib, but he thought he found another spot in the rocks along the canyon wall where another sniper could have as easily covered Terence and the others. It didn't take a tactical genius to position those snipers, but it did show some intent.

The killers had scouted the camp before attacking.

He rose, getting his knees under him, wary of silhouetting himself against lighter rock. Studying the terrain around the camp revealed only Mirabelle going about her useless chores, trying to look busy and not apprehensive. The set to her shoulders told him she would crack under the strain soon enough. He considered the light breeze from the canyon mouth and found several places where someone watching them in camp might hide.

Two of the dark spots proved too shallow but a third was deeper in the side of the canyon, perhaps a cave. He let his eyes adjust to the growing dark as he stared intently at the spot, then moved his head slightly and used a trick he had learned when riding herd. He saw better from the corner of his eyes at night than he did peering straight ahead.

It worked for him this time, too.

Movement. Not much but more than any of the scrubby brush around being nudged by the evening wind. Then he caught sight of a man stepping from the deepest shadows. Slocum couldn't make out the man's features, but he was short, hunched over, and carried a rifle. The dark figure drew the rifle to his shoulder and aimed downward, into camp, at Mirabelle.

That was good enough for Slocum to act. He drew his six-gun and fired. The bright flare of the bullet ricocheting off the canyon wall just below the man's feet sent him scurrying away. Before Slocum could fire again, the man vanished into the night.

6

"John! John! Are you all right!" Mirabelle's frantic question echoed up from below.

"Get down," he shouted. "Don't give him a good shot."

"Who? Is there someone out there?"

"Down!" he roared as he swung his legs over the side of the rounded boulder and slid. He knew what would happen when he hit the ground fifteen feet below.

The shock went up his legs and centered in his injured rib. He almost blacked out as pain hammered at his senses. He gasped, went to one knee, and clutched his side. Through the red haze threatening to make him pass out, he stumbled forward, got his arms around the woman, and used his falling weight to pull her down.

They crashed to the ground in a heap. Slocum was too stunned to keep her from wiggling away and sitting up. They were both covered in mud and ice. The cold worked its way into his bones and helped some to deaden the pain in his side. But not enough.

"You're injured. Did someone shoot you while you were up there?"

"Sniper," he grated out, rolling onto his back. "I did all the shooting. He ran off, into the canyon."

"Toward the gold!"

"He wouldn't bother shooting at us," Slocum said, consciously lying since the sniper had been sighting on Mirabelle alone, "if he already had the gold. He'd hightail it out to California, where nobody'd ask questions about why he had a crate full of gold coins."

"You opened the wound in your side. I see blood oozing through your vest." She pushed back his coat and gentle fingers probed.

As carefully as she explored his wound, the light touch made him wince and almost cry out.

"Do you want me to stop?"

"Yeah," was all he could say. Slocum lay there, gathering his strength and fighting waves of white-hot agony piercing his chest.

He finally conquered the pain enough to sit up.

"I'm going after him," he said.

"But you're injured! You can't hope to fight him."

"He might be one of the gang left to spy on the camp, to see if anyone else would come back. There wasn't enough equipment and supplies for more than one or two unaccounted-for men, so they wouldn't expect to face very many. But now they know you're still alive."

Even as he spoke, he wondered why the dry gulcher had tried to shoot Mirabelle if that were true. They had tortured before to find the location of the gold. Taking her captive would give them the chance to find the location now that the others were dead.

Dead and buried. Slocum got to his feet, aware that he had fallen on top of the mass grave. Nobody under the ground cared, but it gave him an uneasy feeling walking on the grave site.

"I'll go with you, John. You're in no condition to hunt down that man alone!"

He considered all the things he could do—and what wasn't possible.

"You ought to go back to town. Hitch up the horse and return tonight."

"No."

Letting her drive in the dark was chancy. The road was in terrible shape, though dropping temperatures would cause the mud to freeze and likely prevent her from getting stuck in the light buggy. That seemed a better idea than having her tag along as he followed the sniper's trail.

He stood straighter and felt light-headed.

"I'll take the horse," he said. "You'll have to stay here. Will you be all right with that?"

It wasn't a good solution but avoided having to protect her if—when—he caught up with the ambusher.

"There are plenty of blankets from camp," she said in a dull voice. "Can I make a fire?"

He started to say no, then decided there wasn't any reason for her to freeze if he was chasing down the spy. It would take someone as good as an Indian scout to get past him, even in the dark. Still, he wasn't fully recovered and sudden movement sent knives of pain into him, dulling his senses.

"Go on, light a fire," he said. He moved closer and took Mirabelle in his arms.

He wasn't sure what he intended, but it ended up in a kiss that didn't satisfy either of them. With that, he got his horse, took the reins in hand, and jumped on bareback. The horse protested a moment, then settled down, resigned to walking through the dark canyon with a rider weighing it down.

Slocum cast a single glance back. Mirabelle hadn't laid a fire but huddled under blankets at the edge of camp near Ike's grave. A momentary pang for her passed. Slocum concentrated on the man running ahead of him in the canyon.

Listening hard failed to reveal any hoofbeats. He thought the man was on foot, which struck him as odd, but he might have left his horse some distance away, intending to potshot both Mirabelle and Slocum before fetching it. Following tracks in the dark was impossible, even if Slocum could have made out boot prints in the snow and dirt. The canyon began to meander, and only when it branched did he hesitate.

He had no trouble finding the trail. Deep depressions in the snow coming from the canyon branching to his left showed the man had hiked out and then retreated this way. He rode slowly, taking in what details he could. The canyon walls fell away as the bottom widened. Come spring there would be runoff feeding a small stream at his right. Now all that showed was ice turned shiny by the bright starlight. Without clouds, it would get mighty cold fast.

Shivering, he pulled up his collar and hunched over. His horse didn't much like the dropping temperature either, but if they kept moving, they'd both be all right.

Now and then he slowed and even stopped to be sure he wasn't following an animal's paw prints. The trail hadn't been hidden, and this worried him. Looking up to the rocky walls, he saw nothing but shadows cast by overhangs and possible caves. The sniper could be in any of them waiting for the single shot that would take Slocum's life. When the tracks began angling away from the bottom of the canyon toward the distant wall to the left, Slocum turned even warier.

He dismounted and led his horse, even knowing it afforded a better target than he did. Letting it go free or tethering it while he explored wasn't a good idea. He might need the horse to take him out if he ran into a well-aimed bullet.

The fitful wind could not hide the metallic sound of a rifle chambering a round. Slocum moved fast, tugging his horse toward a tumble of rocks. Just as he got the horse to safety, the shot came. The slug tore through the air, too high. The second shot was no better than the first. Slocum drew his Colt, took a deep breath of the frigid air, and then slipped around the rock, keeping in deep shadow the best he could.

More rifle fire betrayed the dry gulcher's position. The bright lances of yellow-orange muzzle flash let him home in like a hawk spotting a kangaroo rat in the desert. When he got to a spot that had to be a dozen feet under where the rifleman lay, he braced his pistol butt against the rock and yelled, "Down here! I'm below you!"

He hadn't expected the trick to work, but it did. The sniper peered over the edge of the rock. Slocum squeezed back on the trigger. The six-shooter bucked once. He heard nothing from above, but he didn't have to. A drop of blood had rained down on him as a testament to his accuracy.

Over the years, he had developed a sense of when he hit his target and when he missed. Taken with the bloody evidence trickling faster down the rock with this sense of rightness, he knew he had sorely wounded the man above him.

Cornered rats fought harder, so he edged along the boulder until he found a way up through the rocks. He had been right to be cautious. As he squeezed between two rocks onto the flat space where the sniper lay, the man rolled onto his side and fired again.

His rifle's report and the one from Slocum's six-gun mingled. A few yards away the sounds would come as one. But being only a couple yards apart, Slocum heard his less powerful one an instant before the rifle. The sniper jerked again and then slid away, his body following the river of blood to the ground below the boulder where Slocum had first attacked.

He stood there a moment, letting the ringing die in his ears. Not sure if he had been shot again, he ran quick hands over himself. The pain in his side came from the earlier wound and not a new one. Squeezing back through the narrow gap between the rocks, he retraced his way to the canyon floor. He kept his six-shooter on the man's dark form although he saw the rifle lying some distance away.

Hideout guns weren't unusual, but his sense again spoke to him. He had killed the man.

Using the toe of his boot, he rolled the man over. Dead. Slocum dropped to his knee and saw that his first shot had taken the man in the throat. The killing shot had drilled through his heart, more by accident than good marksmanship in the dark.

He stood and looked back up the hill in the direction of the canyon wall. The man had come from this spot and had returned. There had to be something around the area that would give Slocum a clue as to the others who had killed Mirabelle's husband and the rest. Picking up the fallen rifle, he examined it. He frowned. The mechanism was rusty. It was a small miracle that it hadn't blown up in the sniper's hands.

Slocum turned uphill and began climbing, following the footprints in the snow and soft dirt. Where the trail crossed rocky patches, the mud from the dead man's boots marked the path as surely as if signs had been put up. The trail opened into a level area. On the mountainside he made out tailings spilling from the mouth of a mine.

There didn't seem to be any other mining activity in the area. Slocum continued following the tracks to a spot where he saw a line shack hidden away in a stand of scrubby trees. The vegetation and side of the mountain would protect the ramshackle building from the worst of the winter storms and in the summer might be cooler than if it had been built out in plain sight.

He shook his head at this. It hardly seemed likely the killer lived here, much less worked a claim. Slocum got the sinking feeling the man he had killed wasn't one of those responsible for the deaths back at the canyon mouth.

Using the rifle barrel, he poked the door, which opened on well-oiled hinges. Inside the dark shack he saw two pallets, one on either side of the room. Between them a Franklin stove pumped out waves of heat. Someone had fed the stove recently. He backed away and looked toward the mine shaft. Faint sounds of digging came out.

Slocum went to the mine and chanced a quick look in. Deep within guttered a single miner's candle. It didn't cast enough light for him to see anything other than rusted tracks for an ore cart and dancing shadows.

"Hello!" His call echoed into the mine and was eventually swallowed by distance.

"Ain't no reason to shout," came the gravelly voice from behind.

Slocum didn't spin around because the prickly feeling at the back of his neck warned him a gun was trained on him. He slowly put down the rusty rifle and kept his hands where they could be seen.

"This your claim?"

"Is. My partner's, too, but he's a lazy good-for-nothing. Not sure where he got off to."

"He tried to shoot me," Slocum said. He turned slowly until he faced a man dressed in canvas pants and a plaid wool shirt. The man wore a strap around his forehead holding an unlit carbide lamp.

"Ain't got money fer the carbide pellets," the man answered Slocum's unspoken question. "Ain't gettin' 'nuf outta this here hole in the ground to stay alive, but me and Bertram do what we can."

It wasn't the smartest thing to do when he looked down the barrel of an old black powder Remington, but Slocum repeated that he had shot the man's partner.

"You kill the son of a bitch?" The heavy pistol never wavered in the miner's grimy paw.

"It was him or me." That wasn't strictly the truth since Slocum could have avoided gunning down Bertram by not pursuing him. Giving more details to justify the killing didn't seem right.

"Never had the sense God gave a goose. Where'd this happen?"

"Not two hundred yards downslope," Slocum said. "You didn't hear the gunshots?"

"Was in the mine. Had to come out to take a leak." The pistol never left dead center of Slocum's chest.

He began estimating his chances of feinting in one direction, diving in the other, drawing and firing before a hunk of shot tore through his chest. It didn't look good. The miner was like a statue, unwavering and not shaking even a fraction.

"I didn't mean to kill him, but—"

"But you didn't have a choice. Bertram always was a hotheaded fool."

"Glad you understand."

"You ain't thinkin' to jump the claim?"

"It's yours by right," Slocum said. "All of it, unless Bertram willed it to next of kin."

"Kin? He don't have no kin, leastways none that'd admit to it."

"You mind pointing that gun somewhere else?"

"This old thing? Hell, it ain't even loaded. I use it to drive spikes in the mine since my hammer broke."

Slocum reflected on how isolation had turned the miner crazy as a loon. That wasn't the kind of admission to make to a man who had just killed your partner and might be interested in stealing whatever gold came from the mine.

"You hear any gunfire a few nights back?"

"Two nights back, yeah, might have. From way off, though. There's folks always pokin' about in these hills."

"Prospectors?"

"Ain't that honest. There's a legend 'bout some damned fool bank robbers hidin' their haul around here. Don't mean nuthin', just a tall tale. Or it might be. Cain't seem to remember 'xactly."

Slocum touched the two coins in his vest pocket. There wasn't anything to tell him Isaac Comstock had found the hidden gold. Others hunting for the robbers' booty might have dropped them. Or some swindler might have salted the area to sell treasure maps or lead a party into the hills to kill them.

The gold coins could have ended up in Comstock's possession in all manner of ways, and with him dead, there was no way to know the truth. All Slocum had to go on was what a grieving widow claimed.

"You see four or five men riding around in the last day or two?"

"Ain't budged from the mine. Found a new vein." The man chuckled. "Might call it a cap-you-lary."

"What?"

"Them's itty-bitty veins. Read it in a book once while I was laid up at a doctor's office. Ain't big enough to call it a vein. Hardly wider than a knife's blade, but it's gold."

Slocum saw the change in the miner's demeanor. He lifted the Remington again, making Slocum wonder if it was unloaded as the man had said before.

"You want me to help bury your partner?" Returning to the other miner's death wasn't too smart, but Slocum wanted to distract the man.

"Hell, let him lay wherever you gunned him down. That's Bertram's rifle. I recognize it. Shoulda blowed up in his face, the way he kept it. I told him to oil his rifle, but he never did. I oil all the movin' parts."

"The hinges on your cabin door."

"You been pokin' in there?"

"Wanted to get my hands warm," Slocum lied.

"You don't want my gold?"

Slocum shook his head.

"Why don't you hightail it outta here? I got work to do. I take the night shift and Bertram does the day work."

Slocum saw that there wasn't much more than single-minded determination to mine gold left in the man. Even acknowledging his partner's death didn't deter him. The isolation had worked its worst and turned the man a touch crazy.

Slocum bade the miner a good evening and started down the hillside, the hairs on his neck bristling until he was sure he was out of range. The only good thing about the night's trek was not having to kill a second loco miner. Somehow, that seemed cold comfort as Slocum mounted and rode back to Mirabelle.

7

It was an hour past noon when Slocum walked into the Damned Shame. The few patrons hardly noticed him, but the barkeep jerked erect as if somebody had stuck him with a pin.

"Slocum, you're here."

"Missed a day or two. Hope that doesn't make a difference. Any trouble while I was gone?"

Beefsteak Malone started to speak, then clamped his mouth shut, his brow furrowed and his rag working frantically on the glass he cleaned. Slocum had never seen the man so agitated.

"I just figgered you was gone."

"Didn't hire anyone in my place, did you?"

"What happened to you?" Malone started to say something else, then scowled some more and finally said, "I mean, you all right?"

"Fine as frog's fur," Slocum said. It was a lie. His side burned as if his wound had been dipped in acid. Riding back with Mirabelle the night before had been something of a chore.

Every hole they hit in the road sent a new pang of discomfort through his body. Riding into the canyon and shooting the miner hadn't done him any good. He wasn't one to cry over spilled milk, but there hadn't been any cause for the miner to shoot at him or for him to kill the man. The miner and his surviving partner had likely both been plumb loco, eking out a living from the played-out gold mine and nothing more. They wanted to be left alone, and when Bertram had come across Slocum and Mirabelle, he had gotten scared.

Slocum only wished his partner had known more about the killers who had slaughtered Isaac Comstock and the others. From the depths of the canyon, he believed the miner when he said that he hadn't heard gunshots, much less the cries of agony as the men were being tortured to death.

"You look a mite peaked," Malone said, putting down the glass and picking up another.

"You already polished that one," Slocum said. He thought the bar owner was going to jump out of his skin.

"Yeah, I have. Why waste effort, right? I ain't payin' you for the days you was off, Slocum."

"Not asking you to," he replied. "My business was mighty sudden and not likely to happen again."

"You tell me if you want to go traipsin' off."

"Any trouble brewing?" Slocum looked around the saloon and saw the regulars already starting to get drunk. Many had come in for the free lunch. One or two might have been so drunk they forgot the food was even there, not that Beefsteak laid out much of a spread.

Slocum helped himself to a couple of the boiled eggs and then took a piece of moldy cheese. He scrapped off the blue fuzz and downed it. He fumbled around and found a nickel for some draft beer. Beefsteak drew it without a word.

Whatever ate at the saloon's owner slowly disappeared by the time the evening crowd filtered in. Slocum thought the man was upset that he had been without a bouncer for a couple nights, though it might have been more than that. Beefsteak didn't strike him as the overly sentimental sort. If Slocum had never been seen again, Malone wouldn't have given him a second thought. As it was, the barkeep kept looking at him out of the corner of his eye in an accusing way.

The piano player showed up and began knocking out songs the best he could on the untuned upright. By the time he had finished his first set, the customers were shoulder to shoulder at the bar, making Beefsteak jump to keep their beer and whiskey glasses filled. He even got a couple cowboys in who demanded mixed drinks, forcing him to show his expertise concocting fizzes and even more exotic libations.

Slocum went to the piano and asked the musician, "How's it been the last couple nights?"

"Nothing special," the jolly, round-faced man said, mopping at his forehead with a linen handkerchief he claimed to have come all the way from France.

"Any trouble while I was gone?"

"Didn't notice you was gone," the man said. He took a sip of his tepid beer. Beefsteak allowed him one free drink an hour. "Must have been 'cuz nothing much happened. No fights or even much in the way of arguments, 'cept for . . ."

"Yeah?"

"Two gents got angry over a card game. Couldn't even tell what they was playin'. Think it was five-card stud, not that it matters."

"Gunplay?"

"One shoved the other. They yelled some shit and then they bought each other drinks until they passed out just before closing 'round four a.m."

"Not very exciting," Slocum allowed.

"Tips have been shit, too." He finished his beer, wiped his lips of foam, and then settled back in front of the piano to begin pounding out "Camptown Races" to get the men het up and drinking.

Slocum drifted around the saloon, listening and talking, mostly finding that Malone was likely the only one who had noticed he'd been gone. Dedicated drinkers, and those not inclined to get into fistfights, concentrated more on the drink in front of them than their surroundings. He doubted any of the men knew anything about him being dry gulched and kidnapped after Rupert Eckerly got himself planted in the cemetery.

He went back to his usual spot at the end of the bar, but Malone still wasn't inclined to talk with him. That suited Slocum. He wanted to watch the crowd for any hint that a customer might be surprised to see him. The gang that had killed Mirabelle's husband and the rest were likely still around—and he thought it had to be them responsible for roughing him up after the funeral.

It was almost midnight when the two men came in, slinking along like weasels. There was a boneless quality to them that caught Slocum's attention almost as much as their secretiveness. They huddled together at a corner table. One drew what looked like a map on the table, only to cover it with his grimy hand if anyone came too close.

They occasionally looked around in such a furtive fashion that he knew they were up to something. Slocum sauntered around, talking to other patrons and moving slowly in their direction. When he got close enough to overhear but not close enough to make them clam up, he took a chair, leaned it against the wall, and sat in it. He tipped back and pulled his hat down as if he was taking a siesta. In the Damned Shame this usually meant a patron had swilled too much of Beefsteak's cheap booze and was sleeping it off.

Slocum strained to hear what the pair whispered. He missed a good deal of what they said, but one spoke louder than the other, and what Slocum overheard sent his pulse racing.

"We kin knock it over, jist like we did them fools outside town."

He missed the reply but almost threw down on them when he heard the response.

"We don't kill none of them this time. I ain't gonna be responsible for any more blood on my hands."

". . . don't worry. This time we'll get the gold and be away 'fore anybody knows it." The man bent farther over the table and used the finger he dipped in beer foam to sketch out a map.

From his position, with his hat drawn down, Slocum couldn't see the map, but as the two worked on it, they became more excited. One's enthusiasm for the crime fed the other's.

"We go for it now," one finally said.

"Now? Won't it be better to wait a night or two?"

"Now," insisted the first man. "You know there's gonna be a guard if we wait till Friday."

The two argued a few more seconds before the wary one relented. They both stood so fast, they knocked their chairs over. Slocum pushed up his hat in time to see them disappear through the saloon doors. He swung forward and righted his chair, then went to the empty table. Two beer mugs were at one side, but the map sketched in the foam was still visible. It took a bit of squinting and not a little imagination before Slocum decided this was a map of Grizzly Flats to the south, where the hotels and whorehouses lined the streets.

He looked over at the bar. Malone averted his gaze. Slocum decided he would quit early. The two were suspicious as hell, and it had been quiet all night long. Maybe not as quiet as the two nights he had missed, but Beefsteak wasn't going to need him for a while. Slocum intended to find out what the two were up to and if they were the ones who had roughed him up. He expected his captors to recognize him, even if he hadn't any idea who they were, but he hadn't given either of them a chance to see him straight on.

Stepping into the cold night from the hot, smoking interior

of the Damned Shame was a punch to his face. He sucked in deep breaths and let the clean mountain air invigorate him. If he interpreted the map right, the two had gone down the main street and then south at the first crossing street.

As he walked, he knew this was the way to his hotel. Mirabelle stayed in his room. He walked faster as he wondered if the two men weren't part of the gang that had killed Terrence and the others and were now on their way to finish off Mirabelle. How they had learned she survived the massacre wasn't something he thought on.

As he reached the front of his hotel, he caught sight of the two men on the far side of the street, keeping to the shadows and whispering back and forth conspiratorially. Wherever they went, it wasn't to his hotel and Mirabelle.

A quarter mile farther, one man grabbed the other's arm and pointed to an isolated two-story house with turrets and a single light burning in an upper window. Slocum edged down the street, watching them. The men ignored anything but the light in the window. They whispered furiously for a moment, then dashed across the street, passing within ten feet of Slocum and never noticing him.

The whiff of booze off the two was almost enough to get Slocum drunk. They crashed into the side of the house, shushed each other, then crept around to the rear of the house. Not sure what to do but curious, Slocum followed. He chanced a quick look around the corner of the house to where the two men stood on the back porch, trying to get into the locked rear door. From the way the house was laid out, Slocum suspected they were breaking into the kitchen.

He doubted they were hungry. Starving men didn't go to such lengths to draw maps in beer foam on a saloon table, then sneak all the way across town to break into a house for a loaf of bread. He hadn't availed himself of the services offered in this house, but Slocum knew it was one of several cathouses.

"Got it!" One man slapped his hand over the other's

mouth to silence him. They spent a few seconds quieting each other, then opened the door and crashed into each other tumbling inside.

Slocum doubted they were two of the gang that had tortured him or killed Mirabelle's husband, but they were up to no good.

Slocum slid his six-shooter from its holster and stepped up onto the back porch so he could look through the open door. The two men were trying to walk on cat's feet to the front room and doing a better job of it than he had suspected was possible from their drunken entry.

This wasn't his concern, but he wasn't going to allow sneak thieves to ply their trade in the middle of the night. Using the butt of his pistol, he rapped hard several times against the doorjamb. The echo through the house was loud enough to wake the dead.

Both men froze and looked at each other, then turned and tried to run. They skidded to a halt when they saw Slocum's Colt pointed straight at them.

"You boys just freeze," Slocum said. "You're not going anywhere."

A soft rustle drew his attention. A tall, well-built redhead came down the back stairs from the second floor, a derringer in hand.

"What's going on?" She swung the small pistol from the two men to Slocum, then quickly turned to cover the two standing with their hands in the air in the middle of the kitchen.

"Seems you've got an infestation," Slocum said. "A pair of rats snuck in to nibble at your cheese."

"Not *my* cheese," the redhead said, laughing. The sound was melodious. For someone who had almost been robbed, she was cheerful enough about the situation. "I charge for any mouse to nibble there."

"I saw them over at the Damned Shame acting suspicious. I trailed them. They broke in and—"

"And it was you rapping, rapping, gently tapping at my window," she said.

"Door," Slocum said, puzzled.

"Never mind. I heard." She came all the way down the stairs. She almost matched Slocum's six-foot height and her curves were in proportion. Slocum could tell. She wore nothing but a thin cotton nightgown pressed against her body by the wind whipping through the door at Slocum's back.

"They intended to rob you."

"My business has been good this week. If they'd waited until Sunday, they might have gotten more from my weekend revenue."

"You got a guard then," blurted the fatter of the two men.

"Now that is interesting. A pair of drunk thieves who actually planned the robbery." She looked at Slocum. "You know my business in this house?"

"Haven't been in town all that long," Slocum allowed, "but I can figure it out. How many girls you got working here?"

"Four. Five if you count the madam."

"You?"

The redhead grinned and nodded. Her coppery hair floated around her pale face. Slocum couldn't tell the color of her eyes, but he would have bet his last dollar they were as green as his own.

"What do you want to do with these two?"

"You're the bouncer at Beefsteak Malone's?"

"I am," Slocum said. "What about them?"

"They should pay for their crime."

"Hands up!" Two gunshots sounded behind Slocum. He spun, only to wince as a rifle barrel crashed down on his wrist. His six-gun went flying.

He heard a rush of feet as the two crooks reversed their course and ran through the house. The crash of a door slamming open at the front of the house warned him they'd escaped.

"They're getting away," he said through gritted teeth. He started to turn and was rewarded with the barrel slamming into the side of his head.

Slocum went to his knees, dazed. He heard boots shuffling around and angry voices. He hardly knew what he was doing but instinct took over. He gathered his legs under him, then launched like a Fourth of July skyrocket. His arms circled a waist and drove the man back to the steps. They crashed down, Slocum coming out on top.

Shouts went unheeded. He was still operating without knowing he even fought. When the rifle barrel slammed again into his head, he sagged, his body suddenly nerveless.

"Kill the son of a bitch," came the angry command.

He heard muffled argument, then the rifle barrel crunched down on the top of his head. His hat robbed the blow of its full fury, but it was still powerful enough to knock him out.

8

The flickering light convinced Slocum he wasn't blind, but he wished he were dead. His head felt like a stove-in watermelon, and where he was bandaged on the ribs burned like a million ants chewed away at him. He tried to roll over but couldn't. It was as if his arms were pinned to his sides. He forced his eyes open and saw a kerosene lamp on a table— on the other side of iron bars.

"You finally back among the land of the livin'? Too damn shame. I hoped you'd up and die on me. There's a shit hole out in the potter's field just waitin' for you."

Slocum levered himself up and let the dizziness pass as he took in his surroundings. The jail cell wasn't the best kept he'd ever seen. Debris on the floor was only part of it. The bars had rusted, and the single blanket covering the straw pallet on the sagging cot had enough moth holes in it to have fed an army of the gnawing pests. Beyond the bars sat Marshal Willingham, feet hiked up on a desk. His bowed legs looked funny with him sitting that way, but what didn't amuse Slocum was the way the lawman played with his six-shooter.

The marshal spun the cylinder, then aimed at Slocum and pretended to fire. Then he'd spin the cylinder again and repeat.

"I got six rounds in the chambers," Willingham said. "Ain't no call for you to bet on whether you get plugged."

"All I need to worry about is when?" Slocum suggested.

"You're a bright guy, Slocum. Too bright. Now, should you be kilt escapin' or maybe there's another—" The marshal cut off his planning when the door opened and let in a cold breath of outside. He dropped his feet to the floor and turned Slocum's six-gun toward Mirabelle Comstock.

"I came when I heard," Mirabelle said, looking at Slocum.

"Now who might you be? You and him, you . . . friendly?" The way Willingham said it made Slocum's skin crawl.

"Why are you holding him, Marshal? He's not done anything."

"Now that's a matter for a judge to decide. Since Grizzly Flats don't have a full-time judge, we got to wait on the circuit rider to come 'round. Might be a week. Might be two. In this weather, he might decide not to come 'til spring."

"What are the charges?"

"Now, missy, I don't know what your interest in this varmint is, but if you ain't a lawyer—*his* lawyer—I don't have to tell you jackshit."

"You can't go 'n lock a man up without chargin' him with some crime."

"I'm the law in Grizzly Flats, and I do as I damn well please. If you don't want to end up in a cell next to him, you git the hell out of my office."

"Is there a bail set?"

Slocum knew Mirabelle didn't have a dime to her name. Or did she? Had Ike found more than the two gold coins and she hadn't bothered to reveal that?

"He's not budgin' 'til I say so. What's your name, missy?"

"I'll be all right," Slocum said, getting to his feet. He leaned against the bars for support. His legs still almost gave way beneath him. "The marshal won't let anything happen to me, will you, Marshal?"

"Shut up, Slocum."

"Do you feed your prisoners? I'll tell the owner at the restaurant to bring him some breakfast."

"Ain't time yet," Willingham said. "Lookee here, missy, you get that pretty ass of yours outta my jailhouse."

"Tell everyone where I am and how I'm staying put," Slocum said. He worried that Willingham would shoot him the instant Mirabelle left, claiming he had tried to escape. "After all, a good and honorable lawman like the marshal here's not going to let any prisoner escape."

Mirabelle went pale when he said that. She understood what was likely to happen. Why the marshal had it in for him, Slocum didn't know, but the murderous intent in the portly man's eyes was obvious. The more people who knew he was in custody and not likely to try an escape, the safer he was.

Willingham fumed at how Slocum tried to box him in. What worried Slocum the most was the chance that Willingham would throw Mirabelle in jail, too, then kill them both in a staged escape.

"I'll be right back, John. Don't go anywhere."

"I won't."

"He ain't gettin' outta my jail alive," Willingham said.

Mirabelle left. The marshal moved to a few feet just outside the cell door, the six-shooter still in his hand. The way he balanced it made Slocum wonder if he wasn't going to kill him inside the cell and then toss in a pistol after the murder to justify his actions.

"You got a big mouth, Slocum. You ain't got no call mixin' that sweet little thing up in your crimes."

"I tried to stop a robbery, Marshal. Ask the woman in the house."

"Madam Madeleine? That bitch would always lie." He laughed harshly. "Hell, that's her business. Layin' drunk cowboys and other degenerates makes her more prone to lie."

Willingham lifted his pistol. Slocum understood the term "shooting fish in a barrel." The small cell gave no place to hide. The marshal could kill him without even being a good shot.

"I am so glad you hold me in such high esteem, Marshal," came a soft voice from behind the lawman. It might have been velvet toned but it carried a knife's edge of sarcasm.

Willingham swung around.

"Oh, do put that silly gun down. You might shoot yourself again. You do remember, don't you, Marshal? How you were showing one of my girls how to do a fast draw and shot yourself in the foot? Who was that? Oh, yes, Jezebel. She's still talking about it. To everyone."

The tall redhead from the whorehouse closed the jailhouse door behind her, took out a dainty handkerchief, and brushed off the marshal's chair before sitting. Slocum ought to have been paying attention to the marshal, but he couldn't take his eyes off the madam. She wore a scoop-neck lime green dress that let her ample bosoms push up in delightful white mounds, almost spilling out. Her coppery hair had been arranged since Slocum saw her last, making her look as if she were ready for a night at the theater, escorted by some wealthy railroad magnate.

Her gloved hands carefully rearranged her long skirts, flashing just a hint of ankle to be wicked. If Willingham had been a couple steps closer, Slocum could have grabbed the pistol from his hands, but Slocum was as engrossed in the hint of trim ankle and the shapely calf above as the lawman.

"He's my prisoner," Willingham said, as if she argued the point with him.

"I see that. What are the trumped-up charges, Marshal?"

"I got plenty on him."

For a moment Slocum worried the marshal had seen one of the wanted posters on him for killing that carpetbagger judge back in Georgia.

"Oh, tell me one. Just one."

"He . . ."

"As I thought. You came running when you found that my house was being robbed. You became confused when this gentleman—Mr. Slocum, isn't it?—so gallantly came to my defense and ran off the two scalawags intent on their criminal ways. I can see how it might happen, it being dark and you seeing Mr. Slocum with his six-shooter drawn and me in my kitchen all . . . in dishevelment after being roused from my bed."

"Your bed?"

"Where I was alone, Marshal Willingham, quite alone. A poor lil' ole thang like me, alone. Imagine that."

Slocum held back his laughter. Madam Madeleine fed the marshal a fantasy that diverted him from wanting to murder his prisoner. Her put-on Southern accent hardly went with her appearance. As if to seal the deal, she lifted her skirts just enough to show her ankles again and crossed her legs in a most unladylike way.

"I caught him red-handed."

"In the act of saving my life! I owe him so much. I am sure this confusion can be squared. Is there any fine he must pay? Bail until the judge arrives? I think Judge Holbein is making the circuit this month. He and I are *such* good friends."

"I heard that," Willingham said.

"Excellent. Do let Mr. Slocum out of that terrible cage." She stood and smiled winningly. Then she said in that razor-edged voice of hers, "Now."

The marshal jumped like he'd stepped in a fire. He dropped the six-shooter on the desk and fumbled for the keys in the top drawer. As he came to let Slocum out, Madeleine scooped up Slocum's holster and six-gun.

"You ain't gonna get away with this," Willingham mumbled under his breath.

"Oh, Marshal," said Madam Madeleine, "he's not going to get away with anything. I assure you of that." She silently handed Slocum his pistol.

It felt good, cold, substantial in his grip. For two cents he would have drilled Willingham and the devil take the hindmost. Madam Madeleine shook her head just enough to dissuade him. Instead of gunning down the marshal, he strapped on his cross-draw holster and pushed past the lawman to leave.

From inside the jailhouse, he heard Madeleine say, "You are such a sweet man, Marshal. Do come by sometime. Jezebel would love to spark with you again."

Slocum didn't hear Willingham's reply but Madeleine said, "Keep going to that hussy Lorelei's house and you'll get the clap so bad your dick will fall off. Do have a pleasant day, Marshal."

She exited the building, looking pleased as punch. She ran her arm through Slocum's and indicated he should escort her back to her house.

"You've got a lot of clout in this town to talk to a lawman like that," Slocum said when they were out of the marshal's earshot.

"Grizzly Flats isn't so large there are a lot of opportunities for men to find female companionship. My house is the best in town, or so I prefer to believe."

"Better than Lorelei's, from what I've heard."

"You don't dip your wick there, Mr. Slocum. Or with any of the other ladies in town. Since you've been here for a couple weeks, I find that strange."

"I don't pay for a woman's favors."

"Ah, I can see why," she said, giving him a once-over.

"Besides, I walked into town with my saddle on my shoulder."

"I know. And that boss of yours is a skinflint, hardly paying what you are worth."

"Is there anything you don't know that goes on in Grizzly Flats?"

"Quite a lot, actually, but I try not to let it bother me unduly if I can't find out. A woman in my position must stay informed."

"As a leading businesswoman?"

"My position is more likely to be on my back," she said harshly. "I don't sugarcoat what I do. I find horny men and extract as much money from them for my favors as possible."

"You look like you'd be mighty good at that," he said.

She laughed. The sound was musical.

"A Southern gentleman to the end, I see. I am good enough that I can employ four other whores. Oh, don't look so shocked."

"Most madams try to make their business sound respectable."

"It is respectable. At least, it's not illegal. I pay my weekly bribe to the marshal for his bogus health inspection. What he gets paid to do and what I *actually* do is just that. My girls are healthy and reasonably happy."

Slocum doubted that. Most soiled doves were addicted to opium or laudanum to kill the pain they felt, both physical and mental. He understood the need to dull what the world did. He preferred whiskey.

Madam Madeleine sighed, causing her considerable bosoms to rise and fall, then jiggle slightly.

"I wish my position in town was more secure. Because of my high standards, most everyone else thinks I am snobbish. Oh, I get plenty of business, but I am not held in any esteem. Grizzly Flats is quite parochial and many here consider me an interloper, my arrival being so recent."

"I appreciate you getting me out of jail," Slocum said. He started to disengage his arm, but Madam Madeleine wouldn't have any of it. She gripped down hard enough to dig her fingernails into his flesh and draw blood.

"We have a few things to discuss," she said.

They entered her house through the front door. Slocum saw that one pane of beveled glass had been broken and a hinge had been pulled free of the doorjamb by the fleeing robbers.

"You want me to fix that up?"

Madeleine raised a carefully plucked eyebrow.

"All that and a handyman, too? I should have suspected." She pointed to a love seat. "Sit there."

The way she spoke wasn't an invitation as much as an order. Slocum dropped into the love seat and watched her go to a cut crystal decanter and pour two drinks. She handed one to him and then sat next to him, her thigh pressing warmly into his.

Madeleine lifted her glass in a toast and said, "To our new partnership." Her emerald eyes fixed on his.

"May it be mutually profitable," Slocum said. He downed the whiskey and wasn't surprised to find that it was much smoother than anything Malone served over at the Damned Shame Saloon.

"You are a cautious man, too, I see," the redhead said. She took the glass from his hand and shifted in the love seat.

Her whiskey-scented breath was hot and sweet as she bent closer. Her lips touched his, a fleeting caress more tentative than he'd expected. Madeleine drew back so she was just inches from him.

"Let's go upstairs," she said. "My bed is all mussed from being roused so early. There's no reason not to muss it further before the maid makes it up."

"No."

For a moment the woman stared. Then she blinked and backed off another inch. Her ruby lips parted, clamped shut, and then she finally said, "You are not joking, are you, Mr. Slocum?"

"You want something else from me. I owe you. Let's get that debt paid before adding others to the bill."

She rocked back and stared at him.

"What do you want me to do?"

"I've never run across a man quite like you before," she said.

"One who turned down your advances?"

"I don't make advances," she said sharply. "Men come to me, begging for what I have to offer."

He said nothing. He had read her right. She had to be in control and used her sex as a potent weapon. Willingham had been more inclined to spill blood—before Madam Madeleine came. She made him forget, at least for a moment, about his blood lust. She thought she could manipulate Slocum the same way. And truth to tell, he was tempted. The redhead was a gorgeous woman, and he suspected she was damned good in bed. If he gave in now, though, he would be forever indebted.

"Is it that woman you're sharing a hotel room with?"

"Mirabelle? No."

"Damn me if I don't believe you." She turned and faced across the room, smoothed out nonexistent wrinkles in her dress, making sure she fluffed up her bosoms to let him know what he was passing up, then continued, "I am tired of those two drunks annoying me and my girls."

"Tell the marshal. He needs something more to do than lock me up."

"I don't cotton much to the law. You understand that, Mr. Slocum, since you are my kindred spirit in that regard. They have tried to rob me before, they accost my girls outside the house, and they never—never!—come in as paying customers. If they did, I would thrash them soundly."

"Tell the mayor."

"Mayor Zamora is an honest man," she said. "My influence over him is small."

"Not like with Judge Holbein."

She smiled at that, one corner of her mouth turning up a little more. She had delightful dimples, but Slocum's resolve didn't weaken.

"He could order them run out of the county, but I want them punished."

"I won't gun them down in cold blood."

"Find them. Drag them back here. I'll take care of the rest."

Slocum considered the situation. He wasn't getting anywhere hunting for the men who killed Isaac Comstock and the rest of his treasure hunting party. And he had no idea where to start in town looking for them, if they were also the ones who had busted him up.

"I'll sweeten the deal."

"How?"

"Your debt to me for freeing you from jail will be erased," Madeleine said. "I can also tell you about the men who abducted you after Eckerly's funeral."

Slocum wondered if she had read his thoughts.

"It's a deal," he said.

"Deal," she agreed. Then she smiled devilishly and added, "Then we can see about other . . . arrangements." She patted his crotch, then stood and walked across the sitting room, her bustle moving in an enticing bump and grind. At the stairs, one foot on the lowest step, she turned and said, "You can go now, Mr. Slocum."

He went.

9

Slocum went into the Damned Shame around noon, after spending some time with Mirabelle, quieting her nerves and convincing her he hadn't shot his way out of jail. She had returned to the jailhouse to find him gone. Somehow, she had missed how angry Willingham was over losing his prisoner. If he had managed to kill Slocum, he would have been happier.

"Heard you was locked up, Slocum," Beefsteak Malone said. "How'd you get out so quick?"

"Raised bail," Slocum said. "Or raised hell. Hard to tell which. Never figured out why the marshal threw me in the pokey."

"Will can be a nervy sort of fellow," Malone said. "I'm surprised he let you out."

Slocum shrugged it off. He had other fish to fry, but he had to ask, "Why's he got it in for me? I ought to have been given a reward, not jail time."

"Will and Madam Madeleine aren't on the best of terms," Malone said. "Might be he thought you two was hangin' out together. He can't do much about her, but anyone carousin' with her is fair game."

"Could be," Slocum said. "It's passing strange, though, the way he's trying to frame me for a crime I busted up and kept from happening."

"You keep the peace inside these here four walls, Slocum," the bar owner said harshly. "Don't go stickin' your nose where it don't belong."

"In Madam Madeleine's business?"

For an instant, Slocum thought the barkeep was going to erupt in rage. The red tide rising in his face subsided and Malone laughed insincerely.

"You got a real sense of humor, I'll grant you that, Slocum. That's why you keep fights from gettin' too bad. Time for you to get to work." Malone pointed to a pair of men at the table near the door, where the trouble had begun last night.

The pair traced their fingers over the sketch on the uncleaned tabletop where Madam Madeleine's would-be robbers had plotted and planned their inept crime. Slocum went over, pulled up a chair, and sat with his back to the bar.

"Howdy," he said.

"We don't want company," the more belligerent of the two said. "This is a private argument."

"Don't care. Bust each other up all you want. If you tell me what I want to know, I'll even buy you a couple drinks."

"To keep me from knockin' this mangy cayuse's teeth down his throat?" The man on Slocum's left half stood, only to be slammed facedown on the table when Slocum grabbed his shirt and yanked hard.

The man recoiled and flopped back in his chair. Before the other man could react, Slocum had his six-shooter out under the table and aimed at his gut.

"Keep it peaceable, gents," he said. "Beefsteak back there makes me clean up the blood on the floor." Slocum glanced toward a dark stain on the boards. "Leastways, the blood I spill. The rest doesn't concern him a whole lot."

"What do you want?" The one on the receiving end of Slocum's Colt growled like a dog, deep in his throat.

"You're sitting at a table where two customers sat last night."

"So?"

Slocum had the pair of them to contend with again. The one whose face he had slammed into the table had recovered and was working up a decent head of mad.

"You've seen them in here before, I'd wager. You were both in here last night."

"Go—" The one with Slocum's six-gun pointed at his gut chopped off his advice when that pistol cocked. To him it must have sounded like the peal of doom.

"What're their names?"

"Don't know their monikers."

"Shut up, Gus. Tell him and we can go about our business."

"Sound advice, Gus. And I really don't care if that business is killing each other, since you're going to take that fight out back." Slocum saw the man waver and then his resolve melted like snow in the spring.

"One's Kel. The other's Malcolm. Herb Malcolm. They're a pair of drifters what blowed into town a month back and stuck like horseflies on flypaper. They spend most of their time down the street in the Lazy Ass Saloon." Gus snorted. "Fits the two of them. Lazy sons of bitches, always cadging drinks and then sneaking out."

"Heard tell they was Peepin' Toms."

"Don't doubt that," Slocum said. He pushed back from the table and holstered his pistol. "You want those drinks or you want to kill each other?" He saw their expressions and yelled over his shoulder, "Beefsteak, these two fine gents deserve a drink on me. Just one, though, since I suspect their thirsts are mighty big."

Slocum backed from the table, spun, picked up the two shot glasses, and dropped the whiskey in front of the men. He went to the door and waved to Malone.

"Back in a few minutes."

"Slocum!"

He let Malone's angry call slide right on by him. There wouldn't be any trouble. The men's rancor would be forgotten until the warmth of the whiskey faded in their bellies. He intended to be back before then.

Walking fast, he went down the street, turned the corner, and made a beeline for the Lazy Ass. He had been in there once, right after he hiked into town and was hunting for a job. The owner had thrown him out, and Slocum had landed the job with Malone less than an hour afterward. That had suited him.

He kicked open the door and looked around the interior. The Damned Shame was usually smoky inside, with everyone puffing away on a stogie or a hand-rolled cigarette. The two went together with serious drinking. Inside the Lazy Ass, men smoked but the air was clear because of the huge cracks in the walls letting through the wind whipping down off the mountains west of town. There wasn't anything a decent carpenter or even a handyman with some caulking couldn't fix, but Randall Cassarian wasn't inclined to spend one thin dime to improve the lot for his customers.

The short bar owner wore a heavy coat and gloves with the fingers cut out against the chill.

The man walked behind the bar on old crates so he would be about level with his customers. Slocum guessed Cassarian might not top out at five feet but he had never seen him outside this saloon and didn't much care one way or the other. Short or tall, the man was bitter and never had a good word for anyone.

"What the hell are you doin' in here, Slocum? Lookin' fer some high-class company?" Cassarian's high-pitched voice cut like a knife. Slocum ignored it and went to the bar.

"Heard tell a customer of yours is owed some money."

Cassarian's eyes narrowed.

"Whatcha sayin'? If any of the lowlifes what come in

here owe you money, that's their business. Either buy a drink or get out."

"I'm delivering some money owed to Herb."

"Don't know anybody named that."

"Herb Malcolm." Slocum took out one of the gold coins Mirabelle had given him and spun it on the bar. It fell to its rim and made a final drop, filling the saloon with the distinctive ring of gold against wood.

"Somebody owes him that?" Cassarian's eyes never left the coin.

"I'm delivering this as a favor. Where is he?"

"Not here. I'll give it to him." The bar owner grabbed for the gold, but Slocum was quicker.

He drew his six-shooter and slammed the butt down on the back of Cassarian's hand, making the diminutive barkeep shriek in protest. Slocum kept the pressure of the butt against the hand and added the extra incentive of cocking the Colt. It pointed straight at the man's face.

"You ain't got no call to do that."

"Just doing my job. Might be, Herb gets generous to the man delivering so much money. Doubt it, but I'm not passing up the chance."

"That's Malcolm, all right. Cheap ass bastard."

"Where can I find him?"

"Outside of town. A mile or two down the road toward Mount Pleasant and a bit south. Him and that no-account partner of his have a camp there."

"You got your wish," Slocum said, letting up on the man's hand. Cassarian tried again to grab the gold coin but he wasn't able to bend his fingers right. Slocum snared the coin and returned it to his vest pocket before slipping his six-gun into its holster.

"What wish's that?"

"You got rid of me. And I got my wish, too."

"Findin' where Malcolm squats?"

"Not having to look at your ugly face." With that, Slocum stepped away, made sure Cassarian wouldn't go for a gun under the bar, then spun and stepped out into the brisk autumn wind.

He turned up his collar as he returned to the Damned Shame to put in his time. Malcolm and his partner weren't likely to come back into town for a day or two. They'd want any trouble to blow over and have Madam Madeleine and everyone else thinking about other, more recent things than them trying to rob the whorehouse.

The rest of his workday and night passed slowly and uneventfully. Slocum didn't even have the satisfaction of throwing the two arguing men out of the Damned Shame because they'd left before he got back.

Slocum had no trouble finding the camp from Cassarian's directions. For a while he thought he was heading back to the site where Isaac Comstock and the others were murdered, but the sight of a small fire off to his left convinced him he wasn't returning to the burial ground. He guided his horse through the darkness and watched attentively for any sign Kel or Malcolm was standing watch for intruders.

From all he had seen of them, he doubted either had the foresight. Even after their failed robbery, they wouldn't be that alert. He rode almost into their camp before he spotted two filled bedrolls near the fire. The blankets rose and fell with the rhythmic breathing of men passed out from too much booze.

Slocum didn't have to examine them to know that. Two empty quart bottles attested to their bender. He dismounted and walked to pick up the first bottle. The label was peeling and faded. He didn't recognize the brand and decided they must have bought this from the Lazy Ass.

"Wha?" The man under the blanket nearest Slocum stirred and sat up. He had a six-shooter in his hand. Slocum took two quick steps forward and swung the empty bottle.

It smashed against the man's head and knocked him flat on his back. The sound of the breaking glass woke the other man. Slocum whirled around and kicked. The toe of his boot caught the man's hand and sent his six-gun spinning into the night.

"You cain't rob us! What've you done to Kel?"

Slocum kicked again and caught Herb Malcolm in the chest. Then he stepped down, pinning him to the ground.

"You must be Herb if that one's Kel."

"Who're you?" Malcolm squinted, trying to focus his bloodshot eyes.

To clear up those eyes, he'd have to cut his own throat and drain them like a swamp. Slocum wasn't about to give him the chance to take any weapon in hand.

"I've been sent for you."

"Sent? Somebody wants us?" Then the import of that sank into his besotted brain. "No, you cain't. You—"

Slocum applied more weight to his boot. Malcolm grabbed at his leg and tried to force him off, but Slocum maintained the pressure until the man passed out.

He looked around the camp and decided there wasn't anything of value—not that he expected there to be with a pair of drifters and sneak thieves. For all their careful planning, they weren't too smart. But then they'd been drunk the night before and they were drunk now. Slocum doubted they strayed much from this state of intoxication.

Finding their horses, he lashed their bridles together, then looped the single reins around the saddle horn on his mount. It took him the better part of fifteen minutes to cut ropes to bind the men's hands. He considered leaving behind their boots, then decided whatever Madam Madeleine intended for these two, he ought to deliver them as intact as possible.

When they'd both recovered enough, Slocum had them put on their boots, then hoisted them to their feet and ran longer ropes from their bound hands to the saddle horn before mounting.

"We got a ways to go, so you'd better step lively. If you don't, you get dragged. I want to be back in Grizzly Flats before sunup."

Kel and Malcolm cursed for almost a mile, then he picked up the pace and forced them to half run to keep from being dragged. They realized he wasn't fooling and would not bother letting them up should they fall. Slocum had set himself a time limit of sunrise to reach town. He bettered that by twenty minutes.

"You—you cain't turn us over to that bitch!" Kel protested. "She'll do us harm!"

"He's right," Malcolm cried. "She'll murder us!"

"Is that so, Madeleine?" Slocum asked when the tall woman strutted out onto the back porch. "You intending to kill these two sneak thieves?"

"Not at all, sir," she said, grinning from ear to ear. "Why, my girls have nothing but special treatment in store for them."

She gestured and four women came from inside the cathouse. Slocum looked them over and decided their employer might be lovely but had lower standards when it came to hiring. Two were fat to the point of waddling. Another made up for it. Her skeletal frame allowed her clothing to flap about her body. The fourth looked as if she was better suited to work the mines. Slocum vowed never to arm-wrestle her. He would lose.

"Give our special guests a good bath, ladies," Madeleine said.

The powerfully built woman stood, looking up at Slocum, and asked, "What about this one? I could just eat him up."

"Now, now, Esther, leave something for me to do," Madeleine said. She laughed at Slocum's wry grin.

The four hookers grabbed the men and shoved them toward a bathhouse. Slocum didn't see smoke curling up from the stove and asked about that.

"Hot water for their baths? Don't be absurd. I'm not going to that much trouble for them." Barely had Madeleine said this than outraged cries came from the bathhouse. Malcolm and Kel were being scrubbed down with water mixed with ice.

Slocum dismounted and hitched up the horses to an iron ring set high on the back wall. Customers likely came in this way, not wanting to be seen entering the front door. Madeleine's four whores came back, pushing the two naked men in front of them.

"My, my, the cold's caused something to shrink," the madam said, looking at two exposed crotches.

"'Twarn't so big to start, but they did smallify real quick," said the scrawny woman.

"Why don't you take our freshly scrubbed guests inside? To the cellar."

"Please, I cain't take more o' this," Kel said, his teeth chattering. "I'm getting frostbit."

"Then you'll like it when my girls warm you up."

Slocum looked sharply at Madeleine, wondering what she had in mind. It wasn't what Kel and Malcolm thought. Both men still shook from the cold, but smiles lit up their ugly faces.

"Down to the cellar," the redhead ordered. A cellar door swung open and the two men were shoved down.

"You want to watch, Mr. Slocum? It can be instructive."

"I've seen Apaches torture their captives," Slocum said.

"Oh, my, no! We're not savages. We are . . . ladies." Madeleine kicked shut the cellar door. "My girls will tie them down, naked of course, then show them how exciting it can be to have a feather drawn all over their bodies. Then they'll soak their feet in saltwater and let a couple goats lick it off."

"After hiking all the way back to town, that sounds a mite painful."

"There's a thin divide between pleasure and pain. Both

of them might just die laughing as the goats have their way with them."

"Might be the goats know them already," Slocum said. This produced a genuine peal of laughter from the madam.

"Do come inside where it's warm, Mr. Slocum. You have delivered what I asked for. It is up to me to give as good in return."

He followed her up the back steps, torn between watching the sway of her bustle and trying to ignore the shrieks of increasingly hysterical laughter coming from the cellar. Somewhere he remembered hearing that this kind of torture had been used by European torturers years back. There were more ways to torment a man than with a branding iron or knife.

"Don't go feeling too bad for them," she said, ushering him into the sitting room. "I am sure they are the ones who peeped through the windows as my girls worked. Once I am sure they spied on me undressing. They are despicable examples of humanity."

"And they tried to rob you."

"Money is replaceable. A woman's dignity is more difficult to mend." She looked at him and shook her head. "You don't believe soiled doves can have dignity?"

"Doesn't seem to go with the job," he said.

"We can, we do. Not all of us, but I prefer to run my establishment in that fashion however possible." She poured more whiskey for him, indicated he should sit in the love seat, and then sank down beside him.

He was aware of the warmth from her leg pressing into his and the exotic perfume she wore. It wasn't applied like most whores. It was more subtle, only a drop or two meant to incite his senses. It worked. He took the whiskey and held it up for a toast.

She clicked glasses with him as he said, "To a job well done."

"That is important to you, isn't it, Mr. Slocum?"

"A man has to live by something. You want dignity, I want to do the honorable thing."

"It no doubt gets you into some real pickles," she said. She sipped at her drink and looked at him coquettishly over the rim. Then she downed the rest in a gulp and gingerly put the empty glass on a side table. "Your honor requires you to find what I know."

Slocum said nothing. He knocked back his whiskey and set the glass on the rug beside his foot so he wouldn't have to reach past her to the side table.

"Very well. You wanted information about the treasure up in the hills. Here's what I know." Madeleine settled back so she could look at him from an angle. Her leg pressed more firmly into his in this position.

Slocum felt himself responding to her warmth, her nearness, then forced himself to concentrate on what she was saying.

"There likely is a considerable amount of gold hidden away in those winding canyons," she started. "Last year about this time, four men robbed a train up north of a large quantity of gold on its way from the Carson City mint to the bank vaults in San Francisco. I never heard the details of the robbery." She primly pressed her skirts flat. "That wouldn't interest you, would it, Mr. Slocum? I am sure you have come up with your own schemes to rob trains successfully."

She watched him for a reaction. He tried not to even blink. This was a woman who accumulated all the tiny details of a man in order to manipulate and control him. The less she guessed about Slocum, the better off he would be.

"A posse immediately formed and chased the robbers into the mountains and all about for some days. Two of the train robbers where killed. The other two were captured some days later, but without the gold."

"They hid it?"

"That is the story. The federal deputy marshal leading the posse had his orders. He strung up the two men."

"And one told the deputy where the gold was hidden in exchange for being released?"

"Astute, but then perhaps you have been in a similar situation. That of the deputy, of course." She still poked and prodded, watching for any response.

"The two thieves were duly hanged. Perhaps one told the deputy where the gold was hidden, but the deputy had a streak of larceny in him. To immediately go to the hiding place meant the others in the posse would know it had been recovered. A small reward might have been offered."

"But the deputy wouldn't be able to collect. It was his job to recover the gold."

"That is the rumor. The deputy knew but returned with his posse to Sacramento."

"And?"

"And barely had he ridden into town than he was shot from the saddle by a jealous lover. Or perhaps it was a man he had arrested at some earlier time. I prefer the story to include a spurned lover. He was taken to a doctor's surgery, where he died."

"A deathbed confession and he told the doctor where to find the gold?"

"That would explain how someone in Sacramento came to know the location and relate it to those murdered out in the mountains, including the husband of the woman you share your hotel room with."

"She didn't know any of that."

"Indeed? Or perhaps she chose not to tell you. The lure of gold might be more compelling than the life of a husband—or lover."

"Who massacred them?"

"Your Mirabelle's husband and friends? Why, that I do not know. It likely was someone in Grizzly Flats since everyone here is always on the lookout for gold coins lying around. The lure of thousands of dollars from a train robbery would be irresistible."

"To you, too?"

"Why, yes, Mr. Slocum, to me also. I am only human. More than this, I have learned to give in to my weaknesses since they are far more fun than anything from my saintly urgings. However, I value some things more highly than I do gold. My freedom, for instance. The chance to determine my own destiny. As you have discerned, I have an overwhelming need to be in control."

"You have any idea who in town might be responsible? For the killings out in the mountains?"

"I cannot help but think whoever kidnapped you after Eckerly's funeral and those killers are one and the same."

Slocum was disappointed. He had come to the same conclusion, but couldn't put any names to the masked men responsible for almost killing him.

"Thanks," he said, getting up. On impulse he took Madeleine's hand and kissed the back, then turned it over and kissed her palm.

"You are a constant source of amazement to me, Mr. Slocum. Do come back when you find the killers—and the gold."

"Perhaps I will," he said.

He reached the door before she called after him, "If you don't find either, do think on coming back anyway."

He stepped out into the light of a brisk, new day and went back to the hotel where Mirabelle slept peacefully.

10

Slocum sat in a chair at the back of the Damned Shame and watched the customers come and go. Tonight was slow, and there wasn't a lot for him to do other than talk to the men and try to get them to buy just one more drink. This part of his job didn't appeal to him. Men shouldn't be enticed into drinking more. Hell, most of them had to be convinced not to drink till they puked their guts up on the sawdust-covered floor. Still, Slocum knew that the better business Malone did, the more likely he was to pay Slocum.

The autumn weather was turning colder as it edged into outright winter, and Slocum considered staying in Grizzly Flats. If he decided that wasn't the thing to do, he had to move on soon. He had taken the two gold coins from Mirabelle to find who had murdered her husband, but the trail kept winding around and coming at him from the wrong direction. Whoever had taken him out into the hills and beat on him were tied into the killings. He was sure of that. If for no other reason than to get revenge on the men, staying in Grizzly Flats seemed likely.

He touched his bandaged side. Mirabelle had done a good

job changing the dressings to keep them from infecting his wound. The shallow crease left by the bullet along his rib refused to heal properly and continued to make sudden movement painful.

Whoever he owed for the wounds, he would pay. In full.

He snapped out of his reverie when Marshal Willingham waddled into the room. His bowlegs seemed more pronounced tonight than before. The man favored one foot as he walked. Slocum had to smile, remembering what Madam Madeleine had said about Willingham triggering the round into his own foot showing off his fast draw. For a man so full of himself, that had to be something he would never live down. Slocum had to wonder what more Madeleine knew about him to keep him in line.

The marshal went to the end of the bar and slapped it a couple times with the flat of his hand. Malone looked sour, then walked the length to bend over to get within a couple inches. He whispered almost a minute to the marshal, who turned red in the face. Slocum slid the leather thong off the hammer on his Colt, sure that the marshal was going to swing at the bar owner.

He didn't relax when Willingham settled down a mite and leaned forward, his face coming even closer to Malone's. The argument went back and forth faster now, neither man monopolizing the talk. When the marshal slammed his hand down hard again, he turned and left without even a glance backward. Malone leaned forward on the bar, head bowed. He finally shoved back and put on a fake smile when he talked to a pair of bank tellers whose only crime was letting their beer mugs go dry.

Whatever argument the Damned Shame's owner had with the marshal never came to an end. Slocum tried to remember how many times the two had had words since he'd come to town. If Willingham had been a customer, Slocum would have cheerfully thrown his ass into the street, but the marshal never ordered a drink. Slocum considered this since he doubted the marshal was a teetotaler.

If his reception at the Lazy Ass wasn't likely to be so choleric, he'd be interested to find if Willingham wet his whistle there. Cassarian wouldn't give Slocum the time of day, though.

He shot to his feet when he saw two men ganging up on a third at a poker table. Standing over them quieted the dispute. One man grumbled about the cards running too lucky for the old-timer across from him.

"Why don't you let the deck cool off and have another drink?" Slocum suggested.

The two gamblers grumbled but left. The old man stroked his scraggly beard, then pointed to an empty chair and said, "Why not take a load off, Slocum?"

"Don't mind if I do." Slocum settled down. This was as good a spot to watch over the peace inside the saloon walls as in the back.

"I heard tell you been askin' 'round about Deputy Underhill." The old man chuckled. "That's where he ended up. Good name. Underhill."

"Don't know him," Slocum said. "He one of Willingham's deputies?"

"Willingham's too cheap to hire any help but his own kin. Them two deputies? Both nephews. He takes the whole amount the town gives him and keeps it. Hell's bells, he don't even patch up that jail of his, but you know that firsthand. You see the rust on the cell bars?"

"I have," Slocum said. "From your knowledge of it, you must know firsthand, too." Small towns were bad when it came to gossip. That was the only entertainment most men in the saloons had, and this old geezer partook of it. "You sound like you're making my business yours."

"Nothing like that. Just that you're a newcomer. Done talked out about all the others in town, 'cept maybe Madam Madeleine. She's not one who's easy to know."

"Unless you have enough money," Slocum said, joking.

"You ain't forked over any money and word is you and her are gettin' to be real good friends." The man winked broadly.

"I did some business for her with the two sneak thieves that—"

"Herb and Kel, yeah, I know 'em. Worthless, the pair of them. Completely worthless. Just like the deputy."

"Who's this deputy you're going on about? I haven't come across anybody named Underhill in town. I might have thrown out a drunk by that name, but I never bother asking for pedigrees before I do."

"She tole you 'bout the gold. That's what I heard."

"Madam Madeleine? She's confiding all this in you?"

"Well, not her but one of her ladies. The one what has some meat on her bones? Her and me, we get together now and again and she tole me you wanted to know about Deputy Underhill chasin' down them train robbers."

"What's your interest?"

"Why, Slocum, I was in the posse. Underhill offered me a dollar a day and a cut of any reward given up by the railroad. Never recovered the gold, and the railroad didn't care that we strung up two of them varmints."

"He came here? To Grizzly Flats?"

"Naw, I was over in Sacramento back then. Worked as an apprentice to a blacksmith." He held out his arm. It bent at an odd angle. "Worked there 'til I bunged myself up too bad to swing a hammer. Deputy Underhill came by askin' for folks able to shoot and ride. I could do that, even if I couldn't hammer out a horseshoe no more."

Slocum listened hard to what the old man said. There was bragging tossed in, but there didn't seem to be any lying.

"Madam Madeleine said the deputy might have been told right at the end where the gold was hidden."

"At the end," chuckled the old man. "At the end of a rope! I watched him dance around, kickin' up his heels. Scared, too, when they put that rope 'round his neck. After his horse got whacked and galloped off, not so much. He tried to talk, and that's when Underhill got all excited."

"What the deputy heard was the reason he was het up?"

"That's the way I saw it. He tole Underhill something. Whispered right in his ear. The deputy lit up like the sun comin' out from under a storm cloud, then he smacked the horse and let the varmint dangle."

"But Underhill took that to his grave. That's what Madam Madeleine said."

"Reckon so, but I was close enough to overhear. Just a bit."

Slocum sat straighter and stared hard at the man. He still didn't hear any lying in the man's voice. But something more entered. Greed. In a way, this made dealing with the old man easier. Slocum understood his motives better.

"Why haven't you gone out hunting for the gold yourself? The deputy's dead. Nobody else would know."

"Have, but not able to get around all that well anymore." He shoved out his leg. It was as twisted up as his arm. "I got kicked by a horse. Busted my knee. Keeps me from riding and ain't no way you're drivin' a buggy out there. And don't even think o' askin' me about my pecker. You don't wanna know, believe you me."

"Why are you telling me? About Underhill?"

"Ain't nobody else in town ever asked 'bout Underhill 'fore now."

"But the gold has been a big topic lately," Slocum said.

The man nodded sadly.

"That loudmouth what come into town braggin' on findin' the gold."

"Sennick?" Slocum had suspected something of the sort.

"Tried to get folks to buy him drinks claimin' he was gonna be rich real soon 'cuz him and the others had found the gold."

"Who kept his whiskey glass filled?" Slocum asked.

"Nary a soul. Folks in Grizzly Flats knowed 'bout the gold for years and that it ain't been found." The old man lowered his voice and leaned forward. "But I know the gold's out there. And I don't think that blabbermouth found it."

"He got himself killed," Slocum said.

"Don't surprise me none. Hadn't heard. Did whoever kill him get the gold?"

"Anyone left Grizzly Flats recently?"

The old man chuckled, then nodded his shaggy head before saying, "You're a dangerous man, Slocum. You think things through. Nope, ain't nobody left, so that means they ain't found the gold!"

Slocum hadn't heard of anyone spreading around money. Grizzly Flats was a town hanging on by the skin of its teeth. If the killers had found the money, they'd be spending it and drawing attention to themselves. It had been their bad luck to believe Sennick. The gold might have been found, but they killed the only man likely to know where it was.

And Isaac Comstock hadn't told his wife.

"That makes what I overheard even more valuable," the man said.

"How do you figure?"

"Somebody was willing to kill Sennick for the gold but didn't find it. That don't mean he's stopped lookin'."

"And you overheard what the robber told Underhill? What would it take for you to pass along those last words?"

"Now you're talkin', Slocum, now you're talkin'. I couldn't get my tongue around the right words for anything less than . . . a case o' whiskey."

"That much?" Slocum said, not doing too good a job of keeping the sarcasm from his tone. The old galoot would kill himself trying to drink that much booze. It would be irresistible.

Slocum just had to be sure the man told him what he wanted before breaking the seal on the first bottle.

"Deal," Slocum said, reaching across the table to

shake hands. The man's grip was weak, and Slocum thought he heard bones grinding together up above the forearm where he had been injured. The glee on the man's face told that he thought the promise of so much popskull outweighed any pain he might feel now.

With a case, he could avoid the pain for weeks.

"I'll be at my place. Just outside town, to the west. When can you get the whiskey?" The old man licked his lips in anticipation.

"An hour," Slocum said, checking his watch. By then the crowd would be gone and Malone would chase him away to keep from paying him one penny more than necessary.

The man scooted his chair back and hobbled away into the cold night. Slocum rocked back in his own chair, watching him go. Getting the case of whiskey wasn't hard. Malone kept a couple dozen cases stacked in the back room, but Slocum thought it was a good idea not to tell his boss what he wanted. Beefsteak had been jumpy ever since Slocum disappeared for the couple days, recuperating from the beating he'd gotten. It was likely that the bar owner no longer trusted him.

That didn't bother Slocum too much. He scented gold—and maybe the answer to who had killed Mirabelle's husband and the others.

"Slocum! Slocum," called Beefsteak. "I got to go for a minute. I musta et somethin' that don't agree with me."

"Want me to tend bar?"

"Don't let these thieves walk off with anything, that's all. After I stink up the outhouse, I'll be right back." Malone walked half bent over toward the back room, arms over his belly.

Slocum vaulted the bar and got a different view of the Damned Shame. It always seemed to him that simply turning around could give a new perspective on life. From here he had a commanding view of the entire room. He also saw three six-shooters stuck into holsters nailed under the bar, as well as the sawed-off shotgun. Malone was ready for anything. Even more than that, Slocum saw the open cash box.

He paused. There wasn't any way the owner could have counted the money yet. However, Beefsteak trusted him not to dip into the till.

"He must be real sick to run off like that," a customer said. "Gimme a beer on the house, Slocum. Beefsteak'll never be the wiser."

"Tell you what," Slocum said, "I'll give you another beer but it's on *your* house."

"You mean I hafta pay! Just like always?"

That got the sparse crowd arguing over whether the customer ever paid and, when he did, it was always late. This suited Slocum just fine. It kept the men entertained and saved him from being forced to improvise some exotic drink asked for now and then. Malone never had a problem as a master bartender with such requests. Slocum didn't know if the man knew the right mixes or if he made them up as he went along.

"You gonna let us stay all night, Slocum?"

"No need for me to say," Slocum answered. "The boss is back."

Malone came from the back room, rubbing his belly.

"Damn, I thought I was goin' up like a skyrocket the way that came out."

Slocum didn't want to hear about the barkeep's digestive problems, but everyone else did. He took the opportunity to slip into the back room and grab a case of whiskey. Dropping it just outside the door, he intended to retrieve it when Beefsteak finally dismissed him for the night. He could pay for the liquor if—when—the owner noticed it was missing.

Twenty minutes later, Malone called, "Down the hatch, everybody. I want to get some sleep."

"That what you call it, cattin' around with that whore down at Skinny Annie's?" This set off a new round of discussion that ended ten minutes later with everyone out in the street and Beefsteak Malone slamming the front doors behind them.

Slocum felt invigorated outside. The air was clean and pure unlike that inside the saloon, but more than this, he was going to get real information from someone who'd been with Deputy Underhill's posse. If the old man wasn't lying.

Walking around the saloon, Slocum fetched the case of whiskey and hoisted it to his shoulder. He wobbled as he walked, the strain on his side more than he'd expected. Anticipation kept him walking steadily toward the edge of town, but he slowed and finally dropped the case when Marshal Willingham galloped past. Immediately behind him ran three men, struggling to match his pace while afoot.

"What's going on?" Slocum called to the one bringing up the rear.

The man huffed and puffed and bent over, hands on his knees as he tried to catch his breath.

"Found Greer dead. Somebody done shot him smack in the middle of the forehead."

"Greer?"

"Yeah, that old fool who hangs around braggin' on how busted up he is."

Slocum let the man lead the way to a hovel about where the old man had told him to go. The marshal's horse stood a few yards away, a man holding the reins. Five others crowded close, peering into the doorway.

Slocum and his guide pushed through the small knot of men. All it took was a quick glance to verify what Slocum had feared. Greer and the man who had ridden with Deputy Underhill were one and the same. From a dim light flickering inside the house, he saw that Greer had taken a bullet to the middle of his face. Blood and busted bone made him almost unrecognizable, but the clothing was the same. And there was no disguising the way his arm and bent leg were thrust out at crazy angles.

"Go tell O'Dell he's got a new customer," Willingham said to the onlooker nearest him. "Ain't no hurry. This one's gone cold already."

An argument began over who ought to tell the undertaker. Willingham chased them away, closed the door, and mounted his horse. He didn't ride back toward his jailhouse but galloped away toward the hills to the west.

Slocum watched him ride off, then had an overpowering urge to find where the marshal was going in such a hurry. By the time he had saddled his horse and gotten on the road, he had lost the lawman.

11

Slocum cursed his bad luck. Willingham had ridden from town like his tail was on fire. Where did the marshal have to go in such a hurry this late at night?

The more Slocum thought on it, the stranger the lawman's behavior seemed. He hadn't been unduly upset over Greer's death. If anything, he was willing to let the body lie there all night long and deal with it tomorrow. The coincidence of Greer's death occurring when it did bothered Slocum even more. If the marshal didn't have anything to do with the old man's death, he knew more about the circumstances than he ought to.

He sat astride his horse, looking down the muddy road. The day had been clear and the bright autumn sun had dried up some of the mud. The temperature had been seasonal, but there wasn't any way he could track the marshal at night on the muddy road. Every hoofprint would slowly vanish as the mud collapsed under its own weight.

Looking into the night served no useful purpose. He turned and headed back toward the hotel, where Mirabelle waited. She was probably asleep by now, so he would risk waking her when he barged in. Taking his watch out, Slocum held it up and caught starlight against the face, reading the time.

Willingham had been gone fifteen minutes. Rather than return to the bed next to Mirabelle, Slocum remained on horseback, waiting in the cold. When he heard hoofbeats, he checked his watch. Almost a half hour had elapsed from the time Willingham had ridden from town.

And sure as sin, the marshal rode back into town. Slocum guessed that he had ridden out, palavered with someone for a few minutes, then turned around and come back to Grizzly Flats.

From deep shadows, Slocum watched Willingham ride past on his way to the jailhouse. When the marshal was out of sight, Slocum checked the watch, got the time, then put his heels to his horse's flanks and galloped off in the direction the marshal had originally ridden. The horse wasn't able to maintain the full gallop long, so Slocum eased back and kept the horse running as fast as it could in the dark along the road.

When the horse flagged, Slocum drew out his watch again. Ten minutes. He slowed the horse's headlong pace and began looking around. Dismounting, he bent over and looked at the road. No one had come this way since the marshal, and whatever hoofprints were visible ought to be his. Slocum slowly followed a track, then saw where it left the road. He studied the area where Willingham must have ridden and saw nothing.

He had an easier time following the fresh tracks once he left the road. By walking slowly, he undoubtedly added to his time compared with the marshal's ride. Then he found a spot where another horse had waited. A pile of dung was still warm. Slocum raised his eyes to the nearest mountain and eased down the slope to a canyon leading into the maze of rocky passages beyond.

He circled the area, reconstructing the meeting that had

gone on here. Willingham came from town to the point he got his horse in a lather, talked with another rider for as much as ten minutes, then returned. The other rider went into the hills.

Slocum swung into the saddle. Willingham had nothing for him. Who had he come to speak to directly from a murder scene? He had no idea if Willingham's ride and Greer's murder were tied together, but there wasn't any disputing how little interest Willingham had shown. Grizzly Flats was hardly a hotbed of crime—until now, until Isaac Comstock's party had arrived. Since then, it had become a bloodbath nigh on as bad as Antietam.

He had difficulty keeping the hoofprints in view, but tracking in such a canyon hardly required him to see anything more than branching canyons. He doubted the rider would take a trail up the steep canyon walls. While there might be trails leading to the rim, Slocum doubted this mattered to anyone meeting the marshal. The canyon floor gave the best chance for finding the hidden gold.

As he rode, Slocum wondered how long the train robbers had wandered these canyons. Long enough to hide their ill-gotten gains, he was sure. He touched the coins in his vest pocket. But had they spent days or hours? If the latter, the hiding place was close to the main road leading to Grizzly Flats.

Not for the first time, he wished that he had delivered the whiskey to Greer and found what the former posse member knew. It might have been nothing more than a ploy to get liquor, but Slocum felt it was more. The old man had known something, but not enough to get him out into the hills to hunt for the gold himself. No matter what he claimed about his arm and leg, if he had known, known for certain sure, where the gold was hidden, he would have come out here. If he'd have to claw his way inch by inch up the canyons, he would come.

Slocum decided Greer had known something—but not enough.

With what Isaac Comstock had discovered, even a tiny hint might have been all it took to find the stolen gold shipment.

He drew rein and looked at the ground. He had a choice of two branching canyons. Even getting down close to the frozen mud availed him little. The tracks might lead in either direction. Making a quick choice, he went to his right, going deeper into the mountains. Before long he came to a small meadow, now cloaked with splotches of snow.

All night long Slocum followed his nose. and by daybreak had to admit he was completely lost. Lost and without real tracks to follow.

Aching and tired from riding all night, Slocum camped. He hesitated to build a fire, then decided if he attracted the attention of Willingham's mysterious partner, so be it. Having the man find him might be easier than Slocum hunting futilely for tracks. He had some jerky in his saddlebags and boiled oatmeal. Then he curled up and fell asleep until distant thunder woke him. He tried to figure out from the sun what time it was, then had to rely on his watch.

"Four," he muttered. He had slept most of the day away, and for what? He had nothing to show for chasing around in the mountains, other than not knowing exactly where he was.

That didn't bother him. He could always follow his own trail back to the road and Grizzly Flats. But did he want to? Mirabelle's problems weren't his. And she had done a good enough job tracking down Eckerly, even if the murderer had died. Her blood lust wouldn't be sated easily, not until all the killers were six feet underground.

That wasn't his fight, even if she had given him the two coins. What ate away at him was being kidnapped and almost killed. The men responsible for beating on him and those who had killed Comstock, Terrence, and the others were likely one and the same. He tried to figure out if this crossing of paths was enough to make him go back to

Mirabelle when they didn't even know how many outlaws needed leaden justice.

The rain pelted down harder. He rummaged about and found his slicker. The half-frozen drops splatted against the canvas and slowly slid off. Shivering, he pulled it closer around him and knew he had to find somewhere to take shelter before his horse froze to death.

He mounted and turned back on his own trail. Slocum tried to remember how long he had ridden, guess how many miles he had come. After crossing the meadow, he came to three canyons slanting off at different angles. By now the rain had erased his tracks.

There hadn't been any hint of the other two canyons in the dark. Slocum tried to reverse his course and figure out where he had come from—and couldn't. With the increasingly punishing rain, being trapped out in the storm would be worse than staying lost. He picked the canyon most likely to have been his conduit into the meadow and knew within minutes he had not ridden this way the night before.

Rather than retrace his path into the teeth of the storm, he kept moving forward and into another meadow, this one rockier and more barren than the one where he had camped. He saw a curious triple peak formation in the distance that he'd never noticed before.

"New territory," he muttered. "Time for a break."

He urged his horse into another canyon mouth and spotted several caves where he might take shelter. The rain fell more heavily and brought down white curtains in front of him. Slocum knew he couldn't take much more of the sleet and went directly to the nearest cave. At first, it seemed little more than a hollow in the wall, but it opened into a decent-sized area after he got past the entrance.

It took some doing to get his horse inside. Slocum took a deep whiff and knew why. Whether a bear still made this its den or had moved on was a problem. Sharing sleeping space with a grizzly was a good way to end up a midnight snack.

Leaving the skittish horse, he worked his way deeper into the cave, hand on his six-shooter. A Colt Navy against a bear was a mismatch he didn't want to have anything to do with, but he had to know about possible neighbors. A small crevice in the rocks showed where a coyote had made a den. Four tiny skeletons told of a poor litter.

After exploring to the back of the cave, he returned to where his horse still pawed at the dirt on the floor.

"Settle down. It's just you and me." He patted the horse's neck and talked to it until its nervousness subsided. It might have been as spooked by the low ceiling and close walls as the old scents.

Slocum took off the saddle and dropped it, then fell to his knees and looked at where the horse had pawed the floor. Even in the dim light he saw a half-dozen golden disks in the dirt.

By the time he finished sifting through the dirt, he had recovered ten gold coins like the ones Mirabelle had given him.

Look as he might, he couldn't find any more—but he did find what had to be blood spatters on the cave wall at about where a man's heart would be.

12

The storm broke an hour before sunrise. Slocum finished what food he had brought, worrying about his horse. When the sun poked above the nearby mountain peak, he led the horse out and hunted until he found a patch of grass, still juicy, if sparse, that provided a decent meal. As the horse ate, Slocum scouted the area, found a notch in the hills behind him that opened onto the curious three peaks he had spotted from the meadow. Although tempted to make a nap, he simply stared at the countryside until he had memorized all the landmarks he could.

Then he walked in the opposite direction, fixing all this in his mind, too. By the time he had done what scouting he could without finding any other cave where the treasure might have been stashed, he mounted and rode toward the rising sun. Every canyon he came to, he chose the branch that kept the sun in his face. After noon, he rode so the sun warmed his back. Eventually he found a way out onto broad plains to the north of Grizzly Flats.

In the distance, from the town, rose lazy curls of smoke, attesting to the windless afternoon. He didn't have to urge the horse to speed. The animal recognized a chance for decent food, water, and a warm stall to spend the night.

Slocum touched the ten gold coins in his coat pocket and tried to figure out what had happened in the cave. A robber must have holed up there, gotten shot, dropped the coins, and then either been taken out or left on his own. The dropped gold had gone unnoticed.

The rest of the loot had to be around that area.

After putting his horse into the livery stable and giving orders for it to be fed and groomed, he paid the stableman with one of his gold coins. This caused raised eyebrows, and Slocum worried he should have bartered awhile longer. He didn't want it getting around town he had come into gold after wandering in the hills outside town.

By the time he reached his hotel, the sun was dipping behind the very mountains where he had wandered lost for a couple days. He started up the stairs when the clerk called out to him.

"Mr. Slocum, she's not up there."

He looked at the clerk, saying nothing. The young man bubbled over with the need to talk.

"She . . . she went with the two men that came for her."

"When was this?"

"Not an hour back. She didn't look happy, but I think she went of her own free will. She, uh, she *is* staying in your room, isn't she?"

"Where'd they go?"

The clerk gestured vaguely.

Slocum hurried on up the steep stairs, taking steps two at a time until he reached his room. The door stood ajar. He eased it open with his foot, though he doubted anyone had stayed to ambush him. Kicking the door shut behind him, he searched the room. Mirabelle's belongings were still in a bag under the bed. His own gear, such as it was, remained untouched in the wardrobe. The woman had been all the two men wanted.

Without more to go on, he doubted he would find Mirabelle easily. Going to Marshal Willingham didn't seem like a reasonable way of achieving anything but being thrown in the calaboose again. Madam Madeleine might help, but he wanted to steer clear of her as long as possible. Not only didn't he want her in danger, but he didn't want to be beholden to her. Finding a couple sneak thieves was likely the least of what she would think up for him as payment for more information.

But did he have any other choice?

Reluctantly he went to the door but froze with his hand on the knob when he heard scratching sounds from behind. He glanced to the mirror above the washstand and saw movement reflected from outside the window. The sun had gone down, erasing any details of the figure trying to open the window.

He stepped through the door into the hallway, drew his six-shooter, and then peered around the door, aiming straight at the window.

When he saw what was happening, he lowered his gun and ran to the window to heave it open. Mirabelle fell into his arms, staggering him. She was crying, shaking all over as he held her.

"I . . . they kidnapped me, John. I got away. They were going to torture me like they did the others."

"You recognize them?"

"No, never seen them before. All I know is they wore masks and one smelled real bad. Beer. The stench was enough to make me gag. And he had a horrible laugh."

He closed the window and shut out the night cold before turning to her. She huddled on the bed, her arms wrapped around herself and her knees drawn up tightly to her chest. Her clothing was plastered to her body so tightly that not even her shivering loosened it.

Whipping up the blanket from the bed and wrapping it around her, Slocum glanced back out the window into the street below.

"How'd you get on the roof?"

"C-Climbed. I got away from them before they could mount. They put me on a horse, then started to mount themselves but I bolted and the horse ran off and . . . and I jumped. I got onto a roof and let the horse run away while they chased after and—"

He held her close to soothe her. After a while the sobs stopped, and she sniffed and controlled herself.

"I didn't know what else to do so I came back here, but they'd find me if I hid in the room. I climbed the drainpipe to the roof and hid there."

"In the rain?"

"Snow, too." Mirabelle sniffed again and wiped her nose on her sleeve. Then she looked aghast when she suddenly realized she had done something so crude.

"I'm not sure how they knew you were here," he said. "I haven't been advertising that fact."

Slocum realized that everyone likely knew he had a woman in his room. What Madam Madeleine knew, anyone could know—for a price. By the time noses were counted and tongues wagged long enough, the rumors would start that it had to be someone from out of town. The men who had killed her husband might likely want to ask after her, just to be sure they hadn't let anyone escape.

More likely, they knew she had escaped the killings and could give them another source of information as to the gold's hiding place.

"I've been so cooped up here, John. It's driving me crazy. But I'm glad I didn't go out, if—" Her eyes darted to the window as if expecting to see her abductors hovering there.

Slocum drew shut the thin curtains, then took off his gun belt, and put it on the washstand. He wrestled with how much to tell the woman about his jaunt into the hills.

"I had a man who was going to tell me what he knew about the train robbers, but he was murdered before I could talk to him." His mind slipped a gear as he wondered if Beefsteak

Malone had counted the cases of whiskey and knew one was missing. Anyone finding it where Slocum had dropped it wasn't likely to ever return it to the Damned Shame.

"So you're nowhere closer to finding Ike's killers?"

"I tried to follow the marshal when he rode out of town."

"Marshal Willingham? Why? He's an unpleasant man but why would you track him down?"

Slocum didn't have a good answer for that, other than the urgency Willingham had shown to leave town when he had been confronted with a dead body. He had been in a powerful hurry. If not to tell someone hiding out in the mountains, then why ride hell-bent for leather the way he had? And then return after only a few minutes?

"He's acting mighty strange," Slocum said. "Doesn't mean anything," he said suddenly. "Forget I mentioned it. Tell me what you can about the men who grabbed you."

"I heard steps out in the hallway, then nothing. I didn't think anything about it until a knock came."

"You answered the door?"

"No. They burst in and grabbed me. The men were dressed like the killers. Dusters, hats pulled down, bandannas up over their faces. All I could see were their eyes. Horrible eyes! Killers' eyes!"

"Calm down," Slocum said, sitting beside her on the bed and putting his arm around her quaking shoulders. He held her until she controlled herself again. When she spoke, her voice was tiny and tortured.

"They took me out the back way so the clerk wouldn't see they were kidnapping me. But he might have seen. I heard footsteps on the stairs from the lobby and thought I caught sight of him."

"He didn't tell the marshal. He said he thought you were going with them willingly."

"Th-They took me down the back stairs, and they had three horses there. Th-That's when I got away. I was mounted and rode and they weren't and—"

He settled her down again. She didn't have much more to add to the story. When she had stopped sobbing, he got up from the bed, strapped on his cross-draw holster, and said, "I'll look out back. Don't think I'll find much since it's been raining."

Mirabelle smiled weakly as she said, "I know." She tried to squeeze some of the rainwater from her hair but her hands shook too badly.

Slocum stepped into the hall, went out the back way, and looked at the ground. The rain hadn't hammered the ground flat, but it had come close. Knowing what Mirabelle had said helped him make out where three horses had stood. Boots and her shoes were mingled into a giant muck pit. Following the tracks from here was impossible. He went back up the stairs and paused outside the door to his room. Staying here wasn't safe anymore, but then nowhere else in Grizzly Flats was any better. He was sure the masked killers were locals, but without proof, he couldn't go around accusing every single last one. He figured Marshal Willingham was mixed up in the deaths.

With newfound certainty, he went into the room. Mirabelle jumped and pulled the blanket up in front of her, as if she could hide that way.

"Get your things. We're leaving town."

"Where are we going?"

"I spent two days wandering around in the hills. I might have some idea where to hunt for the gold, but I got lost. I need your help returning to the spot where Ike gave you the coins. From there I might find . . . my way," he finished lamely. He wasn't sure why he felt so hesitant about letting Mirabelle know he had discovered a few more coins.

"All right. I'll go anywhere with you, John. I feel real safe with you."

He wished he had more confidence that he wasn't riding smack dab into the muzzles of the killers' rifles, but he hid that from the woman. She was shaken up enough from her afternoon of escaping from kidnappers and murderers.

* * *

"How you can see anything in the dark is beyond me," Mirabelle Comstock said. "Without even starlight, we might as well have been riding into the belly of some horrible, huge beast."

Slocum felt the same way but wasn't inclined to let her know he wasn't sure that he was doing the right thing. They had ridden slowly all night under heavy storm clouds threatening to open up at any instant. They had been lucky in that all they faced was the cutting wind blowing off the mountains.

"You up to showing me where you got the coins from Ike?"

"I told you. I can't see a thing, and I have no idea where we are."

"It has to be up that canyon. It's the only one you could have come down into the camp."

"Well, yes," she said, brightening. "From there I turned left. So that means retracing, we go right. I might be able to do this after all."

He let her take the lead as he watched both their back trail and the canyon rim. The last time he had come this way, the old miner had taken a shot at him. His partner was a mite touched in the head, so there was no telling what he might do if he strayed too far from his played-out mine.

"Yes, there," she said, pointing. "Up there! And we walked for almost an hour. I went up to Ike, following his trail."

"How'd you do that?" Slocum asked.

"Oh, John, I can't believe I didn't remember before. Ike left tiny bits of white cloth tied to bushes to mark his trail. He said he was tired of searching the same places over and over. It all looked the same to him, too."

"Might be different in the summer, when there're patches of vegetation," he allowed. "Can you find the trail?"

"Yes, look, there. There's a little bow." Mirabelle lowered her head and turned away. Slocum thought she blushed. "Ike took the cloth from my petticoat. I let him."

He guessed there had been more than tearing strips from her petticoat. He didn't ask. When she was smiling and didn't have that haunted look about her, Mirabelle wasn't a bad-looking woman.

"We're going so much faster than when I was on foot," she said. "There, that canyon's the one where I met up with Ike. I had a picnic lunch with me, but he was so excited. He had found the coins."

Slocum turned up his collar to an increasingly bitter wind. He inhaled deeply and caught the scent of a full-throated storm brewing.

"Let's find the cave fast," he said. "We need to get out of the weather." He brushed snowflakes from his watering eyes. The white specks blew almost parallel to the ground in the stiffening wind. Being caught outside in this would leave their bodies frozen to the spot they stopped.

"I don't know. I wasn't thinking too clearly when I met Ike."

"The gold?"

"I wanted to see him again," she said, her eyes downcast.

"There's a cave that looks big enough for us," Slocum said, heading for a yawning dark opening.

He dismounted and led his horse in, Mirabelle following.

"You watch the horses," he said once they were inside. The cave wasn't too deep, and it would get crowded unless he built a fire. Then they could use the horses to block the mouth of the cave with a fire between them.

He gathered wood and came back to find Mirabelle working to spread blankets. She had unsaddled the horses. The woman looked up and smiled a little.

"This is the cave where Ike found the coins." She held out a small coin. "It was in the dust."

"We can look for more later," Slocum said, using a rock to dig a shallow fire pit. It took the better part of fifteen minutes to get the fire started because of the wind picking up and heavier snow blowing in.

"Feels good," she said, warming her hands on the crackling fire. "Do you think that'll be enough wood to last all night?"

"Better be," Slocum said, looking out into the white curtains drawn back and forth outside the cave. Sometimes he could see fifty feet, at other times visibility was cut down to a few inches.

"We're going to be here for a day or two, aren't we?" Mirabelle said.

"Might be that long," he allowed. He marshaled his firewood and decided he had gathered enough to keep the fire burning at this low level. It would be uncomfortable, but they wouldn't freeze to death.

"Not much food," she said, going through the saddlebags.

"At least we can melt snow for water." Slocum stretched out, his head resting on his saddle as he watched Mirabelle. She finally gave up hunting for food that wasn't there, then began digging through the dirt for other coins.

She gave up after a half hour when no new coins were unearthed. She moved to sit close to Slocum, close enough that she felt the heat from her body more than that from the fire. Holding up the coin she'd found, she let the light glimmer off the gold.

"How much is there supposed to be?" Slocum asked.

"Terrence never said, but Ike hinted that it was thousands of dollars. That'd be at least fifty more of these. I got the idea that there were hundreds of twenty-dollar gold pieces." She handed the coin to him.

Slocum examined it. It was the same as the ones he had found. The words formed on his lips to let her know about what he had discovered while he was wandering around lost, but her kiss snuffed out any talking.

Or his will to talk.

She half lay atop him, her kisses becoming more passionate. For his part, Slocum returned them with fervor. He remembered how she had tended him before, when he was laid up in the hotel room. It had aroused him, but his strength hadn't been enough to go much farther than simply lying back and letting her minister to him. Now he was stronger.

And hornier.

He unfastened his gun belt and cast it aside, then started working on Mirabelle's coat and blouse. All the while they swapped kisses, on lips and cheeks and throat and eyes. As she worked across his forehead, he parted the cloth covering her chest, exposing small, firm breasts. He worked down into the valley between her tits, licking and kissing until she moaned softly.

He caught one nipple between his lips and lavished wet kisses there as he suckled gently.

"Oh, John, I'm on fire. That fills me with so much heat. I want you!"

He worked to her other apple-firm boob and swirled his tongue around. Only when she rose up above him did he leave his delectable post. She sat straight and cupped her breasts, pushing them together a little. They were too small to bounce, but Slocum hardly noticed that. More important was the way he was growing hard—and trapped in his jeans.

"Are you in pain?" she asked, grinning wickedly. "Here?" She reached down and fumbled around to find the lump in his pants. "My, what can we do about this?"

He told her. For an instant she looked shocked, then laughed.

"Ike never used language like that."

"He never wanted you like I do," Slocum said. He was momentarily startled to see the expression on her face. He had inadvertently hit on truth, and it deflated her mood.

Reaching up under her skirts, he stroked over bare thighs and then slipped his hand between them. The heat boiling from her interior spurred him on. She wore nothing under her skirts. He stroked over her hidden nether lips. The change in her expression was instant. Memory was replaced by lust.

Slocum slid a finger into her moist channel, then began stroking in and out until she was thrashing about above him.

Straddling his waist as she did kept him from moving very much.

"In," he gasped out. His erection pained him now as it pressed against his tight jeans.

"Yes, yes," she said. She reached around behind her, fumbled at the buttons on his fly, and finally released him.

The relief was so great Slocum almost lost control. But she moved her hips up, positioned herself, and let him aim upward. Then she simply relaxed. They cried out in unison as he vanished within her tight, hot tunnel.

For a moment, she simply sat, taking his manhood full length into her. He pressed down on the tiny spire at the top of the vee formed by her sex lips. This triggered her hips. She lifted and dropped, letting him slip almost all the way out of her fiery core before crashing down to surround him again.

Mirabelle put her hands on his shoulders and pushed him down so she would have some leverage as she ground her hips down around his fleshy spike. Then she lifted. He arched his back to follow her but she rose faster. When they crashed together, it sent tremors throughout his body. Seeing her bare breasts, the emotions on her face, and feeling the heat and wetness and softness and his own hardness, all tore at Slocum's control.

He moved his hands to her hips to lift and drop her faster. He needed what she was so freely offering and then they found the rhythm that excited them both the most. All too soon, Slocum blasted his seed into her. All around him she squeezed down to milk every last drop from him. Then she sank forward, her bare chest pressing into his body.

It took some shifting, but they finally ended up side by side, arms around each other, as the wind whistled outside. The fire in the pit and the fires within their bodies kept them alive through the night.

13

Slocum came awake to the sound of gunfire. He rolled over a still sleepy Mirabelle and grabbed for his six-gun. The next volley came, and he knew those were rifles. A handgun against a rifle was a sorry way to die. Worse, they were trapped in a cave. Without a back door, a single marksman could keep them penned up until they died of hunger.

Truth was, Slocum's belly already growled from lack of food.

"What's wrong, John?"

"Somebody's firing a rifle," he said. Barely had the words passed his lips when a new round of gunfire sounded. He came to his knees and looked outside the cave. The snow hadn't been as heavy as he would have thought from the storm's intensity. A couple inches had fallen, no more. And the wind had died down, leaving it a perfect diamond-bright day.

He climbed to his feet. Aching legs and side told him how cramped it had been sleeping on the hard rock floor with Mirabelle curled around him through the night. That had been good, sharing heat and so much more, but it made for aching joints and slow movement now. Stretching as he went, he chanced a look around the perfect carpeting of snow. The horses neighed uneasily, but he ignored them and stepped out to get a better idea of what he faced.

The silence weighed on him, then came a new report. He turned slowly and faced the direction of the echo off the canyon walls. No one on their back trail had fired, but some-one up a branching canyon had. Slocum wasn't sure if that reassured him they hadn't been trailed from Grizzly Flats. The two men who had kidnapped Mirabelle had been clumsy. That meant they had a lot to prove to the rest of their gang and that they could make right her loss.

Was finding this cave so important? Slocum shook his head. He was still groggy from the cold night's sleep. The kidnappers didn't know there was nothing more in this cave and likely thought that Mirabelle could take them to the stolen gold's hiding place.

"It's far off," she said. "That's good, isn't it? It means they aren't coming for me. For us."

"Who's being shot at?" While it was possible the outlaws had had a falling-out and were leaving one another dead in the new-fallen snow, Slocum doubted that.

If he'd led that gang, he'd want as many eyes hunting for the gold as possible. Finding it would spark the bloodbath, killing off those who were least able to keep their mouths shut. If the leader was clever enough, he could kill his entire gang and keep the gold for himself.

"The only one you saw was that old prospector," she said. "He was crazy. You said so yourself. Loneliness can make a man do strange things."

More gunshots convinced Slocum this wasn't the surviving miner shooting at ghosts. His expert ear picked out at least two different guns. There might have been a third mixed in, but he wouldn't swear to that. If the miner had decided to shoot at anything moving, it wasn't likely he had more than one weapon.

"His and his dead partner's," Mirabelle said, as if reading his mind.

"Best not to get involved," Slocum decided. She had a good point. Bertram's rusty rifle added to the surviving miner's arsenal, even if it was unlikely he had much ammo. Scratching the walls of a dead mine for the slightest trace of color didn't give them much extra money to waste on ammo and spare rifles.

"I'm getting kinda hungry," Mirabelle said. "There's nuthin' more to eat in the saddlebags."

"Boil them," Slocum said. He wasn't sure what sparked his sudden anger. She hadn't done anything to make him mad. Then he realized he was angry at himself for buying her easy story of the miner's two guns.

"I don't have enough firewood."

He looked at her and saw she had taken him seriously. That made it easier for him, not having to apologize for his sarcastic crack.

"We have to move," Slocum said. "There's no point staying here."

"But the gunfight!"

"It tells me that, if the gang that killed your husband's involved, they haven't found the stolen loot yet."

"It's not here," she said sadly. "Ike must have found almost all there was here. But how'd the coins end up here?"

"I've been thinking on that. The thieves hunted for a place to hide the gold. They might have taken refuge here for an hour or two, then moved on."

"And dropped the coins?"

"It could be they had a tear in the moneybags and never noticed. Chances are good one of them was wounded." Again he held back telling her of the coins he had found in the cave with the bloody smear on the wall.

"Then the gold might be strewn all over the hills!" Mirabelle almost wailed at the thought of losing the treasure.

"I found some more while I was out lost before I got back

to town," he said, finally broaching the subject. She stared at him, her face neutral now. "It wasn't much, but if the bags with the money leaked a bit more, that'd explain the few coins I found."

"How many?"

"A few," he said, not sure why he kept the amount from her now that he had taken the plunge telling her his prior search hadn't been an entire bust. "And there was evidence in the cave of someone who'd been shot. There wasn't a body but blood had been smeared on the wall."

"As if someone who'd been shot leaned against the rock?"

Slocum nodded. She pieced together in a few seconds what it had taken him the long ride back to Grizzly Flats to determine.

"We need to get to where you found it. The rest of the gold's got to be nearby!"

"I looked but didn't see any place where the robbers would obviously hide the gold."

"Can you find the spot again?" She was already gathering their gear and taking it to saddle the horses.

"I remember seeing a mountain formation. Three spires."

"The trident!" she said in triumph.

He stared at her.

"It . . . it was something Ike said. You must have been nearby, where the gold is hidden."

"What else aren't you telling me?"

"The shock of everyone being killed," she said, shaking her head sadly and looking down at the cave floor. "It drove all those memories from my head. Everything is so patchy, so confused. I don't know nuthin' else. Not that I remember."

Slocum wondered if the men who had killed her party would be able to coax more from her by torture. That might be the only way Mirabelle would remember everything—unwillingly.

He finished tightening the belly cinch on the saddle and

mounted. From horseback he carefully worked out a path to the branching canyon that wouldn't leave obvious tracks. If they stayed close to the canyon wall until they changed direction, the outlaws roving these hills wouldn't be as quick to spot them.

Slocum started out, letting his horse pick its own path as they slipped and slid along until there was no other choice but to cut across the canyon bottom and work their way up the next. Landmarks came to him now. This was where he and Bertram had shot it out, and where the miner's partner had remained at their paltry mine. From the tracks in the snow, at least three horses had gone into the canyon. None had come out.

"Keep your eyes peeled," Slocum said. Even speaking in a low voice caused an echo down the canyon. He pointed to the hoofprints in the snow. "They've come in since the storm passed."

"Hunting for me?"

"Hunting for the gold," Slocum corrected. Mirabelle sat astride her horse, uneasily shifting about. He ignored her and kept moving ahead. After less than a quarter mile, he drew rein and studied the canyon bottom.

He had kept close to the wall again to minimize the chance of anyone spotting their tracks, but throughout the area stretching from wall to wall, he saw nothing but chopped-up snow. Impossible to figure out what had happened, he dismounted, drew his pistol, and said to Mirabelle, "Stay here."

"But you'll be out there all alone! They'll see you for certain if they're watchin'."

"Three riders went on, deeper into the canyon where we have to ride. I've got to see why they spent so much time here."

She protested, but he ignored her. He tried to step on exposed stones or in existing hoofprints to prevent anyone from backtracking him to the woman. When he reached the spot where the snow was most stirred up, he saw flecks of fresh blood against the white snow. He looked up and figured that the wounded man had struggled into the rocks on the far side. Slocum worked his way up the slope the best he could. Ice and snow made the going treacherous, and he fell several times.

When he found a larger splotch of blood that had steamed its way down into a snowbank, he drew his six-shooter and listened hard. The wind was still. He heard what sounded like a bellows coming from above him in the rocks.

"You wounded bad, old-timer?" He didn't show himself. The miner had been cantankerous and had just lost his partner. Being shot up by the three men who had left him to die wouldn't improve his disposition any.

"You cain't take my claim. I won't let you!" The miner flopped over a rock and pointed a rifle in Slocum's direction.

Slocum recognized it as the rusty cannon the man's partner had carried. It might not be in good working condition, but if it spat out just one round, it was still dangerous.

"I helped you before. With Bertram."

"Bert? He was my partner till some city slicker upped and kilt him."

Slocum wondered if the miner meant him. He hardly thought of himself as a city slicker, but to a man living in such isolation, he might seem the height of sophistication. In any other situation he would have laughed, but not now.

"You see the men who shot you?"

"Damned marshal tried to gun me down. I ain't done nuthin'!"

"From Grizzly Flats? Marshal Willingham?"

"He's the one."

"He been out here prowling around before? Or the two with him?"

"Surely have. And you ain't gonna take me in on no trumped-up charges jist so you kin take my mine!"

Slocum saw the miner rise from the rock, then lose his balance. He let out a tiny cry as he slid forward over the ice-slick rock, heading straight for the ground. He landed in a heap not ten feet from Slocum.

"You've been shot up pretty good," Slocum said. He saw at least three wounds. From the way they'd bled and stained his shabby coat, there might be another bullet or two in the miner's chest.

"Won't be took into town!"

"How about I take you to your mine and get you patched up?"

"You'd do that? You ain't out to steal my claim?"

"You don't have anything to lose. If I don't get you out of the weather, you'll die right where you're lying."

This small bit of logic made the miner groan out agreement.

"I have someone with me. A woman. She's right good at patching wounds." Slocum waved to Mirabelle across the canyon, motioning her to join him.

He went to see what he could do for the miner until she arrived. He tore back the coat, ripping open a wound that had clotted over. The miner winced but said nothing. The whole time Slocum examined him, he stared hard as if his gaze alone could keep away claim jumpers.

"What can you possibly do for him, John? He . . . he's all shot up."

"I want to find out more about the night your husband was killed. He can tell me."

"How? He wasn't one of the gang, was he?"

"Them folks what got their asses shot off out by the way into the hills?" The miner sagged back, eyes closed. For a moment Slocum thought he had died, but the miner twitched, opened his eyes, and said, "The marshal was one of 'em. Remember his bandy legs, but a lot o' folks have those. Saw him good this time." The miner leaned back and moaned, closing his eyes.

"We've got to go, John," Mirabelle said forcefully. "He's not gonna make it. Look at him!"

"He's tough. We'll take him to his mine."

"They'll get the gold before us! You heard him. The marshal is with them. That makes anything they do all legal."

"Willingham has likely been with them from the start. And there's not much chance they'll stumble on the gold all of a sudden if they've been looking since they killed your husband and his friends."

Mirabelle sputtered as Slocum got his arm around the miner's shoulders and heaved him erect. The man sagged, forcing Slocum to dip down, get under him, and hoist the wounded man upward.

He turned with his burden and went to his horse, letting the miner flop belly down over the saddle.

"From his tracks, there's a trail leading uphill," Slocum said. "I remember this place from before, though the snow makes it look different."

He didn't wait to see if Mirabelle followed. He tugged on his horse's reins and started up the trail marked by the miner's footprints. He recognized the spot where he and Bertram had shot it out and the other man had died. He wasn't going to poke through the snowbanks to see if the miner had buried his partner or just left him where the coyotes and buzzards could feast. It took less than a day for most of the flesh to be eaten away. After a week, the insects had finished their meal, leaving behind a picked clean skeleton. By now the coyotes would have made off with the bones to crack them open for the marrow.

"Don't do this, John. It's wrong. You don't owe him anything."

Slocum ignored the woman's pleas and finally reached a level spot in front of the mine shaft. The miner's cabin was around the outjutting of rock, if he remembered right. And he did. He got open the door and dropped the miner onto the nearest pallet. With his partner dead, he wasn't likely to complain if Slocum had picked the wrong bed.

"Get a fire started," he ordered. Mirabelle stood in the doorway, uncertain. "Now!" His temper was reaching the breaking point. For the time being, they were as safe here as on the trail. Safer. "And fix some victuals. He must have a larder somewhere."

She went about her chore as Slocum pulled away more of the miner's bloody clothing, peeling it away from skin. For all the lead the man had taken, he was in good shape.

"Any whiskey around?"

"A pint. That's all," she said, handing it to him. "I shoulda knowed you was a drinker."

Slocum pulled the cork out with his teeth and spat it across the room, where it bounced off the far wall. He poured a goodly amount onto the worst of the miner's wounds. The man shrieked in pain. Then he passed out when Slocum took out his knife and began digging for the bullets. The blade turned slippery with blood, but the first slug he found wasn't buried too deep. The heavy coat, vest, canvas overalls, and union suit had all slowed it down. It took even less time to worry out the other two slugs. Slocum cleansed the wounds the best he could with what remained of the liquor, then held the bottle to the miner's lips.

"Drink this. You'll feel better."

The man choked but managed to swallow a few drops. He sank back to his bed and began snoring.

"That's a good sign. I told you he was tough. He's going to live," Slocum said.

"If they beat us to the gold, I swear I—"

Slocum silenced the woman with a cold look.

"It's mine. I deserve it, after what all I been through," she said sullenly. "My husband, my friends, all slaughtered like pigs."

"Seems a good comparison. If Sennick hadn't shot off

his mouth in town, you all might have found the gold and then squabbled over it. But he did and they ended up dead."

"The marshal done this. Him and the man I recognized."

"There're a couple others," Slocum said, his mind drifting in that direction. From accounts, Eckerly had just come to town. The others riding with Willingham might have also. Or they could be locals. It didn't much matter since their ambition to get the stolen gold was the same, no matter who they were.

Slocum ate mechanically when Mirabelle put a plate of beans and grits in front of him. If the miner had any meat, she hadn't bothered to put it out. They ate in silence, Mirabelle looking at him from the corner of her eye now and then. He hadn't helped her mood bringing the miner back here to patch him up.

"I'm going to catch some sleep. Join me?"

He wasn't surprised when she shook her head, sank in the corner of the cabin, and drew up her knees so she could rest her head there. Slocum rolled over and had just drifted off to sleep when a cold wind against his back brought him around, six-shooter clutched in his hand. The door stood wide open and the miner was gone.

"What's going on?" Mirabelle rubbed her eyes and looked up.

"He lit out. He's probably out of his head. I'd better go fetch him back."

"Let him go. He's not our concern, John. He's . . . he's an old man and gonna die anytime soon!"

Slocum pulled his coat tightly around him and went hunting for the miner. The tracks were easy to follow—into the mine.

He took a deep breath, touched the cold steel of his Colt, then started in after him. For a fleeting moment, he thought Mirabelle was right. Then he found himself bowled over and fighting for his life.

14

The miner drove the point of his sharpened rock hammer down toward Slocum's face. Caught off guard, Slocum found it impossible to throw the man to either side and to gain the upper hand. He had to match strength against strength. To his surprise, the miner was stronger than he should have been after taking three bullets in his chest. Slocum felt his own power waning. He had ridden too far, been too badly banged up, and hadn't eaten enough to whip even a newborn kitten.

The miner was considerably wirier than that. And being on top allowed him to use his weight to the best advantage. Both hands on the pick handle, he drove it down until it brushed Slocum's forehead. The blade opened a small cut above his eye, but another inch would drive it into his brain.

With a mighty heave that used all his strength, Slocum kicked out and knocked the miner to the side, smashing him into the mine wall. For a moment, Slocum lay there on his back, gasping for breath. He wasn't able to move but the miner did.

With a whoop like an attacking Apache, the miner got

to his feet and ran deeper into the mine. His war cries echoed back to taunt Slocum.

"Are you all right?"

Slocum looked up to see Mirabelle standing in the mouth of the mine.

"I could have used some help."

"He—I didn't know what to do, John."

It rang hollow in his ears. He swung about and levered himself up to lean against the wall. It took several seconds for him to stand. When he did, he was dizzy and a ringing in his ears warned he might have hit his head too hard. He blinked a couple times and got rid of the double vision.

"I'm going after him."

"Why? Let him die in there!"

"He's not in his right mind."

"Neither are you!" Mirabelle called after him as he stumbled along.

The mine was pitch black. Slocum ran his hands along both walls, hunting for a rock shelf where miner's candles might be kept. He remembered seeing the miner with a miner's lamp and saying he didn't have carbide pellets for it. That left only candles for him to work by since no one could possibly find the tiny seams of gold left in this mine by feel alone.

He stopped when his fingers brushed a slick patch on the rock. Slocum couldn't see, so he lit one of his lucifers. In the bright flare, almost hidden by rising sulfur smoke, he saw two candles glued to the rock by melted wax. Prying one loose, he quickly applied the flame to the stubby, blackened wick. A sudden burst of light and then he saw how the mine shaft angled upward. The original miners had followed a sizable gold vein but now only a few sparkles remained to show where it had all been dug out.

"I don't want to hurt you. Hell, I patched you up," Slocum shouted. His words vanished into the depths of the mountain and no reply drifted back to him.

He held the guttering candle high in his left hand, almost scraping along the roof, so he could keep his gun hand free. The tunnel walls were slick from so many picks being applied futilely over the years, but the floor was littered with rocks, some as big as his fist. The miner had brought these from deeper in the mine to examine. Why he hadn't taken them out into sunlight was beyond Slocum.

Another thing that gave him pause was his motive in going after the miner. Let him rot in his own mine. Mirabelle was right. He had already done his duty by saving the miner from the gang roving the hills and digging out the slugs they had put into him.

Being alone too long might have driven the man loco, or he might have been that way before. He hadn't taken the news of his partner's death the way a sane person would have. Slocum wouldn't pass judgment on that score, but he did when he realized his real reason for trying to be sure the miner was all right.

He had killed the man's partner for no reason. Being at the scene of the slaughter, being with Mirabelle and hearing her description, then seeing Bertram had forced him to come to the wrong conclusion. He hadn't any reason to think there would be miners scavenging off the bones of old mines. The only reason he had understood at the time was someone spying on him and Mirabelle to kill them the same way the treasure hunting party had.

Slocum began climbing. A few fissures in the walls and roof showed daylight outside. The mine was crumbling and not too far underground at this point. Then the slope dropped as the mine shaft bored downward into the hillside at a steep angle that forced Slocum to brace himself on the wall to keep from sliding.

After skidding down twenty yards of sloping tunnel, he came to a small chamber where three other shafts went off at odd angles into the rock. The miner could have gone down any of them. Looking for tracks in the dust on the floor availed him nothing since the miner and his partner had tramped through here on a regular basis. Which footprints were recent and which were older would take too long to decipher.

He finally had to admit that Mirabelle was right. He chased a ghost in these mines, and for no good reason. Slocum started back up the incline when he heard the scrape of leather across rock. He threw himself forward and slid back a few feet—and the pickaxe crashed into the rock floor just inches above his head.

Twisting, he kicked out and caught the miner in the gut. The blow lacked any real power, but the wounded man was no match even for this light tap. He sat down heavily and lost his balance on the incline. Slocum heaved himself to his feet and dived forward so his weight crushed the miner to the floor. The impact knocked the wind out of him, but it also knocked out the miner.

A few hard gasps brought him back to regular breathing and good enough condition so he could crawl to the miner. The man looked pale, but he always had from spending most of his life underground. Slocum shook him until the man's eyelids fluttered and came open.

"Who're you?" The croaked question caused Slocum to wonder if the miner was completely around the bend.

"I pulled the slugs out of your chest."

"Yeah, right, 'member that." The miner fought to sit up but couldn't. Slocum had to swing him around so he had his back to the wall. "Thanks," the miner said. He spat out a gob that was black and bloody.

After retrieving the still burning candle, Slocum held it up.

"She told me not to come after you. Damned if I know why I did."

"You get stray dogs followin' you, too, I'd wager," the miner said, grinning crookedly. "Name's Smith, but then, whose ain't?"

"The men who shot you got away," Slocum said. "Why'd they want to ventilate you like that?" Slocum tapped the spots in the miner's chest where the slugs had buried themselves.

"Claim jumpers," Smith said firmly. He scowled when Slocum laughed. "Ain't like that. I'm willin' to let them varmints be, huntin' fer the stole gold."

"You know about that, eh?" Slocum shook his head ruefully. It was time for him to ride on.

"Hell's bells, I know where it's hid."

Slocum held the candle closer to look into the miner's face.

"You know or *think* you know?"

"Me and Bertram been in these here mountains for years. Never thought he'd up and abandon me."

Slocum didn't remind Smith who had killed his partner. At any given instant, the miner sounded rational, then showed lapses of memory and even outright craziness. Which behavior he showed came at random, and Slocum had no way of knowing what would trigger a new bout of running about wildly in this death trap of a mine.

"The stolen gold. Where is it?"

"Cain't rightly say, but I kin show you. Hep me up, youngster."

Slocum caught his gnarled hand and pulled him to his feet. Smith was short enough that he didn't have to duck because of the low ceiling. For Slocum, walking half bent over up the slope and back to the mine's mouth was a chore. If it hadn't been for his battered hat cushioning more than one whack against the low ceiling, he would have been scraped and bloody by the time they reached the mouth of the mine.

Smith took a deep breath of the fresh air when he stepped out of the mine, then choked. He spat more of the bloody gob. From the matter-of-fact way the miner hawked up those gobs, this wasn't anything caused by the bullet wounds to his chest. He likely was dying of consumption. That might be why he was so loco.

Then again, Slocum reflected, some men—and many miners—were better off away from everyone else. They didn't fit well into even the loose society of mountain men or drifters. When it came to the rigid structure enforced in towns these days, they'd go flying off the handle at the least thing.

"John, you found him," Mirabelle said, edging closer from the direction of the cabin. She held Bertram's rusty rifle in her hands.

Slocum took it from her and leaned it against the timbers shoring up the mine.

"Mr. Smith has something he'd like to share."

"I do? Oh, the gold. Yup, I know 'bout that. Me and Bertram roamed all over these hills. I was out huntin' when the posse came gallopin' on the trail of them bank robbers."

"Train robbers," Mirabelle corrected mechanically. She shot Slocum a hot look.

"Whatever they was, they stole. And they hid the gold a couple canyons over in that direction." Smith pointed to the northeast. "Let me show you."

He hunkered down and began scratching what looked like meaningless lines in the dust with his stubby finger. Slocum moved around and began to make sense of the patterns. He jumped as if someone had stuck him with a pin when Smith used three fingers to make a particular mark.

The three needle peaks Slocum had seen when he'd gotten lost earlier were a marker to the gold.

"Here's where they hid the gold." Smith pointed to a line. "Canyon's not too long, but that's got to be where they hid it since they got nabbed real quick afterward and they wasn't carryin' it."

"That doesn't mean a thing," Mirabelle said angrily. She began pacing. Slocum was more attentive to the miner.

"Why didn't you hunt for the gold yourself?"

"What? And leave the Betty Lou?" Smith glanced over his shoulder. "That's what *I* call this mother lode. Bertram, well, he never went along with that. He called it the Louisiana Whore 'cuz he was from Baton Rouge."

"Bet you argued over that," Slocum said.

"Naw, we mostly never spoke out loud. That's how we got along."

"Why didn't you find the stolen gold?" Mirabelle stamped her foot in outright anger now. "Or are you lying?"

"Ain't a liar. Might be many things, but not that. No, ma'am, I figgered we would spend our time better workin' the Betty Lou rather 'n huntin' for gold hid by a gang of robbers."

It made a twisted sort of sense to Slocum. Better the bird in hand than the two in the bush.

"There's a lot of territory in that canyon to hunt," Slocum said.

"'Bout the only ones who haven't scoured it are them vultures that shot me. Damned barkeep." Smith rubbed his chest and winced at the pain.

"What do you mean?" Slocum looked hard at the miner, wanting to shake the words from him.

"He's one of the damned gang what shot me up. He's barkeep in Grizzly Flats."

"Jim Malone?" Slocum asked.

"Never heard him called that. Folks always called him Beefsteak."

"He's one of the gang hunting for the gold?" Slocum's mind raced as he pieced everything together.

The arguments between Willingham and Malone could have been about anything, but they might have been over the gold and searching for it. Slocum had pegged Malone wrong, thinking the man wasn't tough enough to shoot anyone else. If he had been with Eckerly and Willingham when they murdered Mirabelle's husband and friends, he was capable of about anything.

The harder he thought about it, the more it made sense to him. If Sennick had gone to a bar to shoot off his mouth about him and Terrence and the others finding the gold, it was likely the Damned Shame. Malone and the marshal wouldn't have any trouble finding a few bullyboys to join them. The lure of that much gold had driven better men to murder.

"You think them shootists got prices on their heads? Would the marshal pay for bringin' 'em in? I can use a few extra dollars for supplies. Winter's comin' fast and there ain't much gold coughed up out of Betty Lou's throat of late."

"Remember, you said the marshal was one of the gang. I want you—" That was all Slocum got out of his mouth when the shot sang past his head, passing close enough for him to feel the heated lead.

He ducked involuntarily and fell to hands and knees beside Smith. The miner had taken another bullet, this one fatally. Craning around, he saw Mirabelle frantically trying to lever in another round. The rusty rifle had jammed.

"Why'd you do that? You—" Slocum scrambled for cover when he heard the jammed shell pop free and another seat itself in the firing chamber.

Mirabelle shot at him, forcing him to take cover in the mine.

"That's my gold, John. Mine. But if that bartender's one of them responsible for murdering my Ike, I want revenge on him. The marshal, too. I heard what you said about Willingham. I'm going to cut both of 'em down!"

"I can help," Slocum said. He drew his six-shooter, ready to shoot Mirabelle. The thought crossed his mind that everyone hunting for gold went plumb crazy. They might gussy up their motives, but at the heart was insanity, pure and simple.

Another bullet forced him to caution. If he heard her reloading or the rifle jam again, he was ready to rush out.

As much as he wanted to avoid shooting a woman, he would if he couldn't tackle her and get the rifle away from her murdering hands.

But what then? Trying to shoot him broke any bonds there might have been between them. He wouldn't turn his back on Mirabelle Comstock ever again.

"Mirabelle," he called. "I can help you."

"You're not like that, John. I seen how you are. You don't take nuthin' off no one, but you couldn't kill a man in cold blood. I can." She paused, then said in a voice crackling with insanity, "Won't be cold blood when I pull the trigger. It'll be hot blood. I'm so het up now, I might want to rip Beefsteak's throat out with my teeth and then eat his heart!"

Her voice turned shrill.

Slocum suspected he could wait her out. Eventually she would go off, but when she did, she was likely to take his horse with her, stranding him on foot.

He settled himself, then started to burst from the mouth of the mine when he saw the stick of dynamite rolling toward him. Every detail etched itself into his brain. The dull red wax dynamite stick. The black miner's fuse. The sizzling fuse.

The explosion.

15

A powerful shock wave lifted him and sent him skidding back to the top of the incline. Then he slid backward down the slope. The blast exhausted itself above him, saving his life. At the bottom, Slocum lay stunned in the absolute darkness, trying to gather his wits.

He finally sat up and groped about until he found a wall. Using it as a crutch, he stood and worked his way back up the slope. He had cursed this before. Now it served to guide him in the pitch black back to the spot where the dynamite had exploded and brought down the roof. Fumbling about, he cut his fingers on sharp edges of rock piled up and blocking his way out.

Slocum sucked in a breath, held it for a moment, then released it to take another. The air was still good. He wasn't going to suffocate anytime soon, but not having water would do him in eventually. That gave him hours, perhaps a day, to get out.

He began pulling away the rock, only to have more cascade down from the hole above the spot where the dynamite had detonated. Changing his tactics, he worked at the side of the fall, then stopped when he found Smith.

Slocum felt carefully and realized it wasn't exactly the miner he had found. It was Smith's foot, blown off his leg. He knew the man didn't much care since he'd already been dead from the bullet in his head.

Taking a rest, Slocum wondered if Mirabelle had aimed at the miner for what he said or at him. It hardly mattered since she had him trapped. She might well have intended to kill them both. As he sat in the dark, he blinked, then wiped the soot from his eyes. For a second, he thought he was seeing ghosts, then realized a ray of sunlight came into the mine and made dust particles dance.

He heaved to his feet and edged down the mine shaft to the spot where sunlight came through the roof. Slocum looked up and saw that a giant crack had formed a chimney. The clouds in the bright blue sky occasionally blocked the light, but Slocum stood there long enough to get a sense of the size of this chimney and what it would take to edge his way to the surface. He remembered that the tunnel wasn't far underground in some places. This chimney opened at the top of the downslope, so it might be the shortest distance to freedom.

Slocum took off his gun belt, fastened it to dangle under his feet as he climbed, then began working his way up. Back pressed against one side, he reached high and found places to grip. Inching upward, he was glad he had taken off his six-shooter because it got tighter the farther he went.

When his hands stuck out of the chimney and gripped the edge, he could barely move. Repositioning his feet, legs slightly bent, he heaved. And screamed. The pain in his ribs wracked him and the rock clutched at him, as if he had thrust his torso into a cold vise. But as his strength waned, Slocum found resolve. If he fell back, he would never get out. Fingers clawing at rock, toes digging in to propel him upward, he scraped free and got his head above the lip of the opening.

He was looking up the mountainside and couldn't see

back toward Smith's camp, but he worried less about Mirabelle than he did his own weakness. Another surge of muscles brought him to chest level, free of the hole. A final kick
allowed him to flop forward at the waist and take the pressure off his arms and legs. Pain still lanced into his chest,
but he rested long enough to wiggle forward.

Then he had to be sure the six-gun trailing from his foot
wasn't dropped into the mine. Carefully lifting his leg, moving forward inch by inch, he finally pulled both the Colt and
the holster free. Slocum collapsed on the hillside and regained
his strength before sitting up and searching for Mirabelle.

The woman was nowhere to be seen.

He strapped on his cross-draw holster, then slipped and
slid down the hill to land a few yards away from the collapsed mine shaft. Part of Smith's body had been blown
away. He knew where the left foot had ended up—almost
his companion in a rocky, cold, dark grave.

Slocum went to the miner's cabin, then around back. To
his surprise, Mirabelle had left his horse. She had ridden
off on hers, but had lacked the instincts of a thief.

He allowed as to how she could work up from murder to
horse stealing.

Slocum saw her tracks in the snow heading back to the
canyon floor. Tracking her would be easy, but he wasn't sure
he wanted to. He went into the cabin and fixed himself some
food while he warmed his hands by the stove.

He took the time to peel back his shirt and examine his
wounds. He was healing outside, but internally, he hurt like
hell. It might be a month or longer before he felt whole again,
but right now the pain wasn't anything he hadn't experienced
before, nothing a pint of whiskey wouldn't dull.

"Whiskey," he said slowly, as if savoring the liquid in his
mouth rather than the cottony dryness of reality. He had
been too occupied to remember what Smith had said about
Beefsteak Malone.

The barkeep was one of the gang. Avenging the deaths

of Mirabelle's husband and friends took on less a priority in his mind than did getting even with the men who had tortured him. He thought he would have recognized Beefsteak, but the men had been masked. One could easily have been the marshal, with his bowed legs and brusque manner.

The way to find out was to learn a little more, then toss out a lot of lead. Thinking of evening the score with Malone and the others caused Slocum to instinctively reach over to touch the ebony butt of his six-shooter.

As filled with warm food as possible and feeling better from the brief rest, he got up, went to his horse, and started down the trail for Grizzly Flats.

The town didn't look any different, but Slocum felt a coldness now that he never had before. Men here would torture, rape, and kill to recover stolen gold. That made everyone he saw on the street a little more distant, a little more dangerous. He knew a couple of the men and had to use that knowledge to find the entire gang.

He considered leaving his horse in the livery, then decided that would announce his return as loud as riding down the main street firing off his six-gun. Almost of its own volition, the horse turned toward Madam Madeleine's cathouse. Before he had dismounted, the rear door opened and the red-haired madam stood with her hip cocked and one hand there to emphasize her curves.

"Didn't expect to see you back looking like you were pulled through a knothole backwards," she said. "Thinking on spending some time? I've got just the girl for you."

"Only you'll do," he said, dismounting. Slocum tried to sound light, but her response seemed sincere.

"For you, anytime."

"I need to use your barn for a spell," he said, slapping the loose end of the reins across his palm.

"So that's how it is. That'll cost you," she said.

"What doesn't?" He fished in his coat pocket and found

one of the gold coins retrieved from the cave floor what seemed an eternity ago. "This'll do?"

"Honey, for this, you can stable your horse and ride me for a week."

"Quit tempting me."

To his surprise, the lightness had left his words. He looked at her, their green eyes meeting for a few seconds longer than comfortable for either of them.

"You have to be in a passel of trouble, Mr. Slocum. It figures I'd go for a man like you. All I find is trouble."

"This can work itself out pretty quick," Slocum said.

"A liar, like all the others." Madeleine looked disgusted and pointed to the barn. "Do what you have to there, but if you get shot up, don't come crawling to me. I don't want to get blood on my fine sitting room rug."

"I'll bleed out here," Slocum said, some of the joking returning. She didn't take it that way. Madam Madeleine slammed the door, leaving him to wonder at the woman.

He doubted she acted this way toward all her customers, but the twenty-dollar gold piece should have made her mood a bit straightforward. Pondering this, he led his horse to the barn and tended it with a good currying and some grain in a nosebag while he considered how best to approach Beefsteak and the marshal.

Somehow, thoughts of Madeleine kept intruding, making his plans jumble up. He finally left the barn, walking slowly through the twilight. Grizzly Flats was closing down for the day, and the saloons were brimming with customers. Licking his lips made him yearn for just a taste of whiskey, but going into any saloon would get back to Beefsteak Malone in a flash.

He kept to the shadows and worked his way toward the jailhouse without being seen by anyone. The door stood open a fraction and cigarette smoke billowed out. Some of the smoke reached Slocum. His nostrils flared. A bit of whiskey would go down warm and smooth. A smoke now would be good, too.

His desires took backstage to more immediate needs

when two men rode slowly toward the jail, looked around before dismounting, then finally lashed their mounts to the iron ring set in the jailhouse wall and went inside. A final backward look around told Slocum these two men weren't going to see Willingham on any legitimate business.

He crossed the open space and got to the cell window set high in the wall. Straining, he barely made out the voices. Willingham did most of the talking, with only occasional replies from the men. That told Slocum who was in charge at the moment, though he had to believe Beefsteak Malone was their actual leader. The times he had talked with the marshal came closer to argument than conversation. Willingham didn't like it that someone else was calling the shots.

That might be a wedge to jam between the men, though Slocum wasn't sure how he could use it.

The only words he could make out clearly were Willingham's.

". . . don't screw this up. She's got to know where to find it."

A bit of mumbling from the others, then Willingham concluded, saying, "You git on outta here. Carson seen her, then the fool lost her. She knows more 'n we suspect."

Feet shuffled and the door slammed. Slocum looked around the corner of the jail and saw the pair walking their horses down the street, heading for the Damned Shame. Neither of them entered the drinking emporium, though. One went around the side of the building and the other sat heavily in a chair in front, rocked back, and pulled down his hat, as if sleeping.

They knew Mirabelle was coming and had set a trap for her.

Slocum decided it would serve his purposes if he caught the woman before Malone's gang.

Going around the block and finding the alley behind the saloon, Slocum saw how the outlaw had positioned himself. It was almost as if he wanted to be seen, but Slocum doubted that. The man had only contempt for his quarry and figured she would never bother looking around before trying to enter the back way.

If Mirabelle tried, the man would come up from behind the rain barrel and grab her.

Slocum walked on cat's feet until he was only a yard from the crouching man. Something gave him away, possibly the way his boots made small sucking sounds as they moved in the half-frozen mud.

Rather than turn to face him, the man surprised Slocum by driving himself backward from his crouch. His face was up to the sky, but his shoulder found Slocum's knees and sent him staggering away. The outlaw hit the ground, rolled, and came to his feet before Slocum could recover.

"What the hell's your problem?" Slocum growled. "I wanted to go into the saloon and you knocked me over."

"You snuck up on me."

"Didn't see you," Slocum said, getting to his feet.

He didn't give the man the chance to ask why anyone entered the Damned Shame through the rear. Rearing back, he unleashed a haymaker that connected with the man's belly. The shock was enough to knock the man back but not hard enough to put him out of the fight. In a flash they were swinging at each other, each giving as good as he got.

One hard punch to Slocum's breadbasket almost ended the fight. Pain lanced into his chest and made him gasp. He fell forward and grappled with the man, pushing him to the rain barrel. For a brief instant, the man was off balance. This gave Slocum the chance he needed to reach down, grab a kicking leg, and heave upward.

The outlaw went headfirst into the rain barrel. Slocum heard a crunch as the man's head broke a thin layer of ice, then came gurgling. There couldn't have been more than a foot of water in the barrel, but it was enough to drown in. Slocum grabbed both kicking legs and made sure the man didn't get his nose above the surface of the icy water. A final convulsive kick and then a motionless body assured Slocum the man was dead.

Panting harshly, he stepped away. Then he realized he could have found out from the man important details of the gang. Looking at the bright side of it, though, Slocum was still alive and damning himself for killing his enemy, while one of the gang was permanently removed.

Slocum turned over the barrel and pulled the man out, then went through his pockets. A few silver coins, a watch that didn't run, and what might have been a map were all he found. Carefully unfolding the soggy paper, he tried to decipher what had been on it. The pencil lines were all smeared and the paper itself fell apart as he handled it.

He wadded it up and dropped it on the man's chest. He still had another source of information out front.

Getting to him would be a little harder, but not much.

Stride long, he rounded the corner of the saloon in time to hear the chair where the other outlaw had waited fall to the boardwalk.

A commotion from inside the Damned Shame warned him that he was in for a whale of a fight. Slocum went to the swinging doors and peered over the top to see the guard from outside the saloon hanging on to Mirabelle's hand, keeping the gun she held pointed at the ceiling.

It discharged a couple more times before the man finally knocked it from her grip.

She turned and attacked like a wildcat.

Slocum knew better than to go to her aid. Beefsteak held his shotgun and would cut down anyone interfering. Better to let them take Mirabelle out back, where they thought the other man waited.

He rushed around the saloon to the alley, hand resting on his six-shooter. The instant both the outlaw and Malone stepped out, he would have them both in his sights. Slocum waited—and waited.

He counted to ten and then to fifty and knew they weren't bringing her out this way.

Not knowing what had gone wrong with his plan, he

returned to the front of the saloon to see the outlaw still fighting with Mirabelle. She clawed and kicked and tried to bite him. He shoved her hard into the middle of the street. Slocum made a move to intervene when he heard Marshal Willingham and Beefsteak Malone arguing.

Both were just outside the saloon on the boardwalk, Beefsteak with his sawed-off shotgun and Willingham with his six-shooter drawn. Slocum did a quick calculation and knew he could never bring down both men before the third gang member drew and shot him.

If he went for the man in the street standing over Mirabelle, either Malone or Willingham—or both!—would fill him with enough big holes for a blind bat to fly through.

"We don't want to make a big ruckus," Malone said.

"Too damn late for that," Willingham said. He waved his six-shooter around and even swung it in Slocum's direction.

Slocum ducked back, but the marshal was only gesturing wildly.

"I'll lock her up."

"I can't leave the saloon," Malone complained. "Business is too good tonight. Always is just 'fore a storm hits. Ever'body wants to get likkered up to ride it out."

"There's no hurry," Willingham said. "She ain't goin' nowhere, not once she's in my cell."

"She better be there, Will. I swear I'll cut off your ears and cram them up your ass if you try to cross me."

"I'd never do a thing like that, Jim. You know it."

Slocum wasn't sure how that sounded to Beefsteak, but to him it was a huge lie. And that suited him just fine. He waited for Willingham and the other outlaw to drag Mirabelle away, still struggling. He only had to deal with the two men, not three.

And when Beefsteak Malone showed up at the jailhouse thinking he was ready to find where the stolen gold had been hidden, Slocum would be waiting for him.

16

Slocum started after Willingham, his deputy, and their captive when a ruckus inside the saloon burst out into the street. Slocum half turned, then hightailed it across the street to get out of sight. Beefsteak Malone had his shotgun out and was swinging it around wildly. If he had spotted Slocum, he would have cut loose with both barrels.

In the middle of the street two men fought like wildcats, hammering at each other with fists as hard as stone. From their looks, they were miners, fit and tough and determined to make the other pay for whatever slight had gotten them ejected from the Damned Shame. With Beefsteak Malone watching over them, Slocum had no chance to pursue the marshal.

He kept to the side of the building, holding his breath, as if Malone might somehow hear or see or smell it.

The two miners continued to fight but weakened quickly. Slocum had never seen a real fight last longer than a couple minutes. Either the men intended to kill each other, in which case it was over quick, or they only wanted satisfaction and not the other's death. Most fights were about bragging rights and humiliating the opponent. If the other fighter died, there wasn't any way to lord it over a corpse.

Malone made sure no one from the saloon interfered, but he also swung his weapon around to fend off anyone elsewhere in the town coming for a bit of entertainment at the drunken men's expense. More than one citizen of Grizzly Flats walked in front of Slocum, intent on the fisticuffs.

"All right, git up, you two jackasses," Malone said finally. He lowered his shotgun, went and grabbed one filthy, mud-covered man by the back of his coat, and lifted him to his feet. The other he kicked a couple times to get moving. "I'll give the two of you free drinks—but nobody else!"

A groan of rejection went around those who'd watched, but several helped the fighters back into the saloon. Beefsteak stopped and looked around the street, motioning to the onlookers who weren't filing inside to join the festivities. A couple did.

As far as the Damned Shame's owner was concerned, the two free drinks for the fighters brought him more customers and an hour of rehashing the fight between those not taking part.

Slocum waited for the swinging doors to stop flapping back and forth before pursuing the marshal and his captive again. He didn't quite run but came close. Catching Willingham and his deputy off guard mattered. Otherwise, there'd be more dead bodies littering the streets of Grizzly Flats, likely his. He slowed his rush when he caught sight of the jail and then stopped.

The door was closed. But no smoke curled up from the stovepipe sticking out of the roof at a crazy angle. Willingham didn't strike him as the sort to suffer the cold when the wood or coal was paid for by taxpayers' money.

He slid his Colt from the holster, held the weapon at his side, and advanced cautiously. He pushed gently against the door. Latched. Slocum eased up on the wood peg in the latch, got it free, then kicked the door inward. It slammed hard against the wall and rebounded, but by then he was inside and pressed against the wall to the side of the door.

His six-shooter swung about just as Malone's shotgun had—but he had no one to sight in on. The jail and cells were empty.

Slocum swung around and looked outside at the doorstep. His were the only tracks coming in atop a light snowfall. He hurried around the calaboose and saw where horses that had been tethered were gone, leading off toward the mountains to the west of town.

Willingham and his deputy had taken Mirabelle back to the site of the massacre to force her to tell them where the gold was.

Slocum started for Madeleine's and his horse when he heard two men arguing as they approached the jail from the direction of the Damned Shame. One of them was Beefsteak Malone. Slocum flopped down behind a watering trough that had cracked from the ice in it and leaked into a puddle just under his face.

"Should never o' let them take her, Beefsteak," complained a man Slocum had never seen before.

"Didn't have no choice, and you were gettin' soused down the street."

"Got to keep an eye on the competition," the man said without any hint of apology. "It was up to you to keep an eye on Willingham. You knowed he was intendin' to double-cross us."

"I don't know that bitch can tell him anything. If she wasn't in the camp the night we hurrahed it, she could have been collectin' the gold. But I doubt it. Otherwise, she'd have taken it all and we'd be none the wiser."

"She might have the gold and still want revenge for killin' her friends."

"No," Malone said positively, "I read people better 'n

that. She wanted revenge—and she don't know where the gold is."

"So what do we do about the marshal and that no-account deputy of his?"

"They're likely headin' for the canyon where they shot up that old miner what interfered. We can start there."

Slocum knew what Beefsteak Malone meant. They had filled Smith with three slugs and then ridden away to let him die. The search for the gold had to pick up there with Mirabelle's help, willing or otherwise.

He stepped out, leveled his pistol at the back of the saloon owner's head. It was an easy shot. He could kill him for the kidnapping and torture after Eckerly's funeral, then get off a couple more shots before his partner knew what was happening. Before Slocum could squeeze back on the trigger, a half-dozen men came down the street, yelling and waving to Malone. Slocum lowered his pistol.

His chance for a clean kill was gone. If he shot Beefsteak and his crony now, he'd have half the town coming down on his head in a matter of minutes. He slid his pistol back into his holster and walked away. If Malone was right, he knew where to start looking for Willingham and his captive, too.

After all, Smith had died there from Mirabelle's bullet, and Slocum had almost been permanently entombed by her stick of dynamite. It was hard to forget a place like that.

By the time he reached the barn behind Madeleine's, the snow blew into his face and made his eyes water. Riding in this storm would be hard. He slammed the barn door behind him and felt the chill knife wind stabbing between the boards.

"You won't last a mile in this storm," came the soft words.

He spun, hand reaching for his iron. Slocum relaxed when he saw the madam at the back of the barn, a heavy blanket pulled around her shoulders. She shivered a little in spite of the blanket, and then he saw why when it opened just a tad in front. Slocum had thought Madeleine was also wearing clothing underneath.

She wasn't.

All he saw was milky white skin and a rusty red patch nestled between her thighs.

She quickly pulled the blanket back around her body, covering up the peep show.

"You won't last so long either, dressed like that."

"You mean undressed," she said, opening the blanket again and walking forward slowly. The blanket trailed behind her, but all Slocum could see was the way her body moved like a lithe, muscular mountain lion.

"I'll lose them in the storm," he said, but his argument felt flat and bitter against his tongue.

Madeleine came closer until she was only a few inches from him. Her breasts had tightened with the cold. He saw gooseflesh on the firm, snowy cones. The nipples turned into hard bright pink pebbles as a new gust of wind blasted through the wood panels in the door.

"You know they'll be slowed, too, and you know where they're going," she said.

"Did Willingham pay you to slow me down?"

The look of anger that flashed on the woman's face told him the answer before she spat it out.

"He hates me, and I don't think so highly of him either. Since I came to town, he's done everything he could to put me out of business."

"Why?"

"I refused to let him have so much as a caress without paying for it. I'll pay him cash money as a bribe but that's all he'll ever get from me." She reached out. Cold fingers touched his cheek, moved lower, then worked between his shirt and skin. She stepped a little closer so her breasts pressed into his chest.

"You could leave town," Slocum heard himself saying. Blood pounded in his ears, almost drowning out her reply.

"I intend to. One of my girls run off to get married. Another killed herself yesterday. An overdose of laudanum. The two left aren't worth the dynamite it'd take to blow them to hell."

"But you could make a good living by yourself."

"So good of you to say that, Mr. Slocum, but I find myself doing things that aren't very businesslike." She pressed insistently against him now.

He kissed her. After a satisfactory length of time they broke off and pulled back, their lips almost touching.

"I find myself wanting to give away the merchandise to a select customer."

"How often?"

"Only once," she said. "Now."

This kiss lasted longer. Slocum's arms closed around her, and they began to slowly spiral about, a sexual dance that caused her to rub against him like a cat. Her legs parted enough so she could lock her thighs around one of his. She began rocking up and down. After almost a minute of this, coupled with passionate kisses, Slocum felt his jeans getting damp with her juices where she rubbed the hardest.

She was ready for him. He had been ready for her since she had come toward him clad only in the cold night air.

He reached around her, cupped her ample, fleshy buttocks, and lifted. Her legs spread for him, and she locked her heels together behind his back. He kissed her lips and cheeks and throat. As she leaned back, his mouth worked lower to the deep canyon between her tits.

He stopped kissing for a moment and asked, "That hurt? My beard's got to be like sandpaper."

"I love it, John, I love it. I want more!"

She clung around his neck, pulling herself forward to bury his face between her marshmallowy mounds again. He enjoyed this, but his tight jeans robbed him of some enjoyment. She knew this instinctively. Dropping flatfooted to the straw, she ran her hands down his body, across his belly, to unfasten his gun belt and then his fly. Her quick, knowing fingers unleashed the hidden monster.

His manhood snapped out, long and hard and proud. He gasped when she took just the tip into her mouth as she knelt in front of him. Her tongue whirled about like the storm winds blowing outside, then suddenly left.

She tugged on his jeans, working them down.

Looking down at her made him desire her all the more. She swayed from side to side as she worked at his pants, her breasts jiggling as she moved. He ran his fingers through her fine spun copper hair and pushed it away from her face. She looked up at him, emerald eyes blazing with lust.

Or was it more? He couldn't tell. And then he found it hard to think coherently. She took him in her mouth again and grabbed a double handful of his ass flesh as she rocked back into a stall.

He followed her down, his cock never leaving her sucking, demanding mouth. Her fingers worked between the meaty slabs of his ass and toyed with what she found. A quick finger drove into him and massaged, stroked, worked against his insides, and made him so hard he cried out.

"Now, John, now you're ready." Madeleine scooted up, pulling the blanket with her so she could lie back on it.

Her legs parted wantonly, exposing her nether lips invitingly. He dropped between those sleek legs and let her grip his erection and guide him to the pinkly scalloped gates to paradise.

She arched her back and drove him balls deep in a single thrust. They both cried out at the sudden intrusion. Slocum felt as if he was being squeezed in a wet, hot vise. She tensed and relaxed her inner muscles in ways he had never felt before. Then she sank back to the straw. He followed her rather than slipping free of such a fine berth.

Supported on his locked arms, he stared down into her lovely face. A few freckles marred the skin—or did they add to her beauty? He began moving insistently, driving deep and hard, unable to hold back. She had done so many things to arouse him he couldn't back off now, even to rest. He saw a flush rising in her cheeks and spreading down to her throat and lower.

The tops of her breasts turned rosy and then he closed his eyes as sensations overcame him. She lifted her knees on either side of his driving body and rubbed against him. He sank deeper with every thrust until he was sure he would split her in half. She took every stroke and gave back as good as she got by squeezing down all around him.

They fell into a mutual rhythm that built their emotions to the breaking point. Slocum tried to hold back the fiery tide that began in his balls and then inched along his shaft, but the sounds, the feel, the way Madeleine knew all the right places to touch and pinch and stroke, caused this slow advance to become a heated rush.

His spilled his seed, and it vanished into her greedy heated core. All too soon Slocum felt himself melting in her inner heat. He sagged down, winced, and realized he had wrenched his ribs again.

"That was something," she said in a husky whisper. "Now hold me."

Slocum moved around to lie beside her, then rolled and pulled the blanket up over their tightly pressed bodies. A relaxation descended on him that made it possible for him to forget his aches and pains. She felt vibrant and warm in his arms, the anodyne for what had been ailing him for so long.

"It's hardly fair," she said. "You're still mostly dressed."

"Not where it counts," he said.

"Oh, here?" She reached between his legs and caught at him with those strong fingers.

He recoiled, expecting her to clamp down hard, but she

surprised him again with a gentle stroking that caused life to stir within sooner than he would have expected.

"There's no rush this time," she said. "The storm's going to blow all night long."

"Will it?"

She slithered down and took him in her mouth again to show how enduring this storm could be.

17

Slocum stirred, then came awake with a start to see Madeleine standing with her back to him, peering out a small window in the wall. He wanted to stay like this as long as he could. Her back was creamy smooth and flawless. Her hips were wide and her waist trim. Most of all he liked her shapely legs.

As if she sensed him watching, she looked over her shoulder and gave a smile that combined shyness with a touch of earthiness. He knew what she did for a living—and he was willing to admit she did it well. But there was a vulnerable part to her that he couldn't explain.

She bent, giving him an added treat, picked up the blanket, and settled it around her shoulders.

"It's cold in here," she said.

"That's because you got up. You should have stayed here beside me."

Madeleine smiled, this time with a touch of sadness.

"You have to go after them, don't you? No, don't answer. I'm good at reading people and see it in your eyes." She went to the window, used the edge of the blanket to wipe away frost, and looked out. "I need to go, too."

"Back to the house?"

"No, I'm going to leave Grizzly Flats. I've overstayed my welcome here." She laughed harshly. "What little welcome I ever had. Folks here never cottoned much to me. I could never figure out why." She shrugged. "Things like that happen."

"Where'll you go?"

"Doesn't matter. 'Not here' is as good a destination as any"

"What will you do? The same?"

"Hardly. I'm good at this, but I'm good at other jobs, too. I worked as a teacher for two years. Then I dealt faro for six months. There's not much I don't know about the law, even if I can't practice as a lawyer."

"You've led quite a life," Slocum said, sitting up. He shivered and wondered how she kept from freezing with only the blanket around her. Her bare feet on the dirt floor ought to have sucked every bit of heat from her body and frozen her like a marble statue.

"We could compare what we've both done, what we've both seen," she said. Her shoulders slumped. "But you have to go kill the marshal and Malone and who knows who else?"

Slocum didn't bother answering. That summed up what lay ahead for him. He got to his feet, buttoned his fly, and strapped on his six-shooter. He stood behind her, hands on her shoulders, and looked out the window. The snow wasn't as bad as the wind had suggested the night before. That suited him. Plowing through two feet of new-fallen snow was both difficult and dangerous. With the couple inches that had fallen, he might not find the trail easily, but knowing where Willingham was likely to have taken Mirabelle Comstock, he didn't need signposts to follow.

"There's plenty of food in a crate over there," Madeleine said, pointing. Slocum followed the line of her slender arm, then bent and kissed along it. She drew back, hiding it under the blanket. He tried to part the blanket, but she held it tightly closed. "Better get on the trail, John. If you don't go soon, I'll try to make you stay. And you will and will hate me for it."

Slocum was sure she might try to lasso him, but she overestimated her charms. He was harder to keep in one place, but she was right about one thing. He might stay a bit too long and lose Willingham and the others. For a moment he wondered why he bothered with Mirabelle after she had tried to kill him—and had killed the miner.

She was out of her head with grief, he decided, and he hadn't been focused enough on avenging her husband. Slocum's lip curled slightly into a sneer. What Willingham and the others in that gang had done to him was enough to keep him on their trail. He touched the injured ribs. In spite of the aggressive acrobatics he and Madeleine had engaged in the night before, he felt mighty good. Perhaps that was the best medicine for what ailed him.

"Go," she said. The redhead bowed her head slightly. Slocum saw a tear on her cheek. Before he could say anything, she brushed it away and said again, "Go on. Get out of here."

The crate with the food was more than he could ever stuff into his saddlebags. He took enough to last him a week, saddled his horse, and led it to the door. Wind had blown snow through the cracks. The morning sun lit the frozen cracks and made it look like a primitive stained glass window. Putting his shoulder to the door, he swung it open against the drift.

The blast of cold air took his breath away. He mounted, gentled the horse, and got it moving away from the barn. Before leaving the yard, he looked behind him to see Madam Madeleine watching. She waved, then turned and darted back into the barn. Settling down in the saddle, he got his bearings and headed west. The crystal clear air showed the mountains ahead and even gave him a different route into the maze of canyons.

If he intended to find the gang, he had to return to the

cave where he had found the coins that still clinked together in his pocket. He almost turned and went back to the barn. Paying for the food was within his ability now, and he had simply taken it, though Madeleine had urged him to do so. He had given her a twenty-dollar gold piece earlier, and that ought to cover it.

Slocum realized he was hunting for reasons to return to the fiery redhead when duty lay ahead.

Duty and revenge.

He settled down and rode for the canyon he suspected led back into the hills where he had seen the three peaks. Mirabelle had not paid much attention when Smith scratched that in the dirt, and she wasn't about to give up any other information quickly. Knowing what Willingham and the others had done to the rest of Mirabelle's party, she would be tortured and hold out.

For a while. She would hold out until they convinced her with enough pain to reveal what she knew. What she didn't know she couldn't reveal. Every minute the killers from Grizzly Flats were delayed, the better Slocum's chance of finding them and rescuing Mirabelle.

He rode steadily, the weather finally aiding him. He kept a sharp lookout for other riders and tracks in the freshly fallen snow. It was as if he were the only man in the entire world exploring virgin territory. This settled his nerves and reminded him why he enjoyed being on the trail alone. There was a serenity out here he never found in any town crowded with noisy, obnoxious cowboys and settlers. Individually, they were decent company but together they crowded him. Out here he was free.

The wind kicked up a mite and bit at his face. He pulled up his bandanna to protect his nose and mouth. Even through the cloth he smelled the dampness. Another storm was on the way. The sky was crystal clear and scrubbed of any clouds, but he knew he had to find shelter before sundown or he might be frozen into a statue out in the open.

As he made his way up the canyon floor, he slowed, then cocked his head to listen hard. The windy whine made it difficult to be sure, but his keen ears picked out the sounds of horses. A quick look at the snowy ground assured him that the riders hadn't come this way. That meant they'd entered the canyon from another path, likely going past Smith's mine—where the gang had ridden before. They systematically hunted for the spot Slocum already found.

Ahead at the far end of the canyon he saw the three peaks rising like stony fingers prodding the sky.

A shout echoed down the canyon. The words were muffled and undecipherable, but Slocum knew the gang rode toward him. He looked down and saw no way to conceal his tracks to this point, but finding refuge might keep them from getting on his trail since the sun was fading fast behind the very trinity of peaks he sought.

Cutting to his left, he kept his horse on the rocky patches. This made the going more treacherous since a thin layer of ice turned them slippery as hell. He reached the canyon wall, looked up, and saw nothing but long shadows cast back in the direction he had come.

No obvious caves presented themselves for him to hide. Slocum dismounted and led his horse to a large rock that had fallen from above at some time far in the past. He tried to decide if there was any current danger. The ice and snow formed an overhang that could cut loose with a small avalanche at any moment. Not seeing any other spot to hide, he moved his horse closer to the boulder, then tied the reins to dead brush before sidling along the rock to get a better look into the canyon.

Two men rode along. One used binoculars to scour the canyon walls. Slocum wasn't sure what they hunted, but they would certainly spot him in a few more minutes if they kept riding.

He caught his breath as the pair stopped to argue. Snippets

of their words came to him. The one with the binoculars wanted to quit hunting. The other insisted they go on. The first made an argument that set Slocum's teeth on edge.

". . . we can use that sweet li'l thing Willingham caught in town. She looks like she'd be a whole lot of fun."

"For you, the fun'd be over in a couple seconds," joshed the second.

"Says you. You and that there whore—she kicked you out of a cathouse!"

This retort cut to the quick and went beyond joking, at least for the man without the binoculars.

"Go to hell."

"Naw, I'll go back to camp. Don't freeze out here, 'less that's the only way you'll ever get hard enough."

Slocum saw the second man reach for his sidearm, then relax. There had almost been bloodshed. That would have improved the odds for him. Depending on how good a marksman the one was, it could have removed both men. A wound, a shot back, a prolonged exchange—Slocum wanted both men to fill each other with lead.

Just like they had the miner. Just like they had Isaac Comstock's entire party.

Slocum missed what the one with the binoculars said, but the man tucked them into his saddlebags and then wheeled about to return up the canyon floor. For a moment Slocum thought the other outlaw would join him, but the man spat and kept riding.

This was the worst thing that could have happened. He came across Slocum's tracks within minutes. Stopping, the outlaw scouted the entire rocky face, then slowly homed in on the boulder where Slocum hid. The man drew his rifle and rode forward slowly, bringing the rifle to his shoulder in anticipation of firing.

Slocum was trapped. He couldn't mount up and ride. There wasn't much cover for him to launch a protracted fight. With sudden determination, he slid his six-shooter from its holster, held it just a little behind him, and stepped out, waving with his left hand.

"Hello!" He cursed the way the canyon funneled his greeting and carried it in the direction taken by the other outlaw. He walked fast in the direction of the approaching rider, needing to reduce the distance as much as possible so his six-gun would be as accurate as possible.

"My horse pulled up lame. Can you help me?"

"Surely can, mister," the outlaw said.

Slocum lifted his Colt and fired at the same instant the rifleman did. His slug went wide, but he corrected and began fanning the hammer. Three more rounds missed, but he finally hit his target. The outlaw only got off a second shot before being hit. Worse for him, his horse reared and threatened to unseat him.

Walking steadily, Slocum knew he had only two more shots before he'd be up shit creek. The outlaw fought a wound in his left forearm and a skittish horse.

Slocum fired again. This slug ripped through the man's thigh and buried itself in the saddle leather.

"Son of a bitch!" The outlaw wobbled, then fell from horseback.

One more round rested in Slocum's six-shooter. He had to make it count.

"Don't want to shoot. Throw away the rifle."

"You're gonna kill me no matter what." The man flopped about, dragging himself through the snow and mud, half rolling down into a ravine.

Slocum heard the rifle chamber another round. He could take cover himself or he could attack. Without conscious thought, he let out a rebel yell and charged. This spooked the man into firing too fast. Then it was too late for him. Slocum was on top of him, his finger coming back on his trigger. The gun bucked, the man died.

Slocum charged past, skidded on the slippery slope, then

came back. His bullet had gone smack through the man's hat and into his head, killing him instantly. He damned his bad luck. He could have gotten information from the man if he hadn't died like this. Slocum had no idea how many were in the gang, where their camp was, and how Mirabelle was being held.

Slipping and sliding, he went back to the downed man and searched his pockets, hoping for a map or something more he could use. Other than a few dimes and a silver cartwheel, there was nothing useful.

"What'd you find? You signalin' me?"

The echo came from the direction the man with the field glasses had ridden. In the dark, those binoculars would do him no good, but Slocum had not thought to grab the dead man's horse. It ran wildly up the canyon, toward the approaching outlaw.

He reached the spot where he had left his own horse. It pawed nervously at the ground, upset at the gunfire. Slocum swung into the saddle and decided on a frontal assault. He might just bluff his way out of this.

All he needed was a pair of brass balls and a ton of luck. He rode down the slope past the man he'd killed. He saw the dark figure of the other outlaw. He'd come to a halt a hundred yards away.

Slocum waved his hat, then slowly closed the distance between them, keeping his head down so his hat brim hid his face. In the gathering dark this probably wasn't necessary, but Slocum had to get as close as possible before revealing himself.

"What'd ya find?"

Slocum mumbled and cut the distance between them in half.

"Cain't hear you," the outlaw said, growing restive. His horse swayed back and forth, as if unsure which direction to run.

"Found it," Slocum mumbled.

He didn't know what gave him away. The outlaw jerked out his rifle and began firing wildly. The rounds went past Slocum, warning him not to come closer. He decided to carry out his plan of charging into the fusillade aimed at him, hoping to spook the rifleman. Just as he tapped his spurs against his horse's flanks, he saw two other riders coming to reinforce their partner.

Slocum ducked down, put his shoulder into his horse's neck, and turned it. Only when he was facing away did he let the horse have its head. Bullets from more than one rifle chased after him.

18

As he rode in the darkness, Slocum worried over the terrain and where the canyons he had passed led. He counted on knowing the mountainous ways better than the outlaws because he had gotten lost here and had found his way out. At the time that hadn't seemed to be beneficial, but now it was.

He veered to the left, found a ravine, and rode in it, keeping a low profile. Then he slowed and finally stopped, listening for sounds of pursuit. He heard angry calls and recognized Marshal Willingham's strident voice immediately. Two of them were on his trail. Thoughts of ambushing one, then taking on the other, were born and died immediately. He didn't have the ammo for a prolonged fight. For all he knew, Willingham had his saddlebags filled with boxes of cartridges.

The two didn't work together well, giving him a second thought of dividing them and finishing them one by one. Then he heard Willingham's hoarse whisper.

"Keep shoutin' like you don't know where I am. We'll take him."

"Cross fire?" came the second outlaw's raspy voice.

Willingham's reply was too low to be overheard, but he knew they'd laid a trap for him. If he had blundered into an attack, they would have shot him down.

Urging his horse across the canyon, he got to the far wall, followed it to a branching narrow corridor or rock. He had seen this before and had avoided it. Riding down it, his shoulders scraped the walls. The closeness caused his horse to rear and try to back out. He gentled the horse the best he could and kept it moving forward. The way was entirely cast in darkness. He trusted there wouldn't be any sudden drop-off. Even a few feet might prove fatal for him and the horse.

The horse let out a whinny of relief as it burst out from the rocky corridor into a valley. At the far end he saw the three spires of rock dark against the last light of day. He pulled his horse to the left and found the mouth of the canyon where Willingham and his partner still sought him. With a bit of luck, they might get lost and return to their camp too late.

Slocum grinned when he saw the flicker of a campfire not a half mile off. By the time he caught the scent of burning pine, he was within a hundred yards of the outlaws' camp. Mirabelle had thought there were four. He figured there were at least six. He had gunned down Eckerly and drowned the one behind the Damned Shame in a water barrel. A third had died at his hand back in the canyon. That left Willingham and likely his deputy—and at least one in the camp holding Mirabelle prisoner.

Finding a ravine that meandered past their camp, he dismounted, drew his six-shooter, then carefully reloaded. Only then did he advance. The smell of grub cooking made his mouth water and belly growl. It had been too long since he'd had anything worth eating.

If he had been thinking straight, he would have eaten breakfast before leaving Grizzly Flats, but Madeleine had jumbled up his head. If he had to choose missing out on the night with her or a full belly, he'd go hungry for a month of Sundays.

"You surely do cook up a tasty mess o' beans," Beefsteak Malone said. "I ain't had this good in a spell."

Slocum heard a soft, feminine voice reply. The words were lost in the crackle of the fire. He moved to the bank of the ravine and chanced a quick look over the rim. Mirabelle sat with her back to him. That explained why he couldn't hear her words. Malone sat on the far side of the fire, forking in the beans she'd fixed for him.

If he could have crept over the edge of the ravine, he would have gotten the drop on the outlaw straightaway. As it was, he had to work to get up. That would give Malone plenty of time to go for the six-shooter shoved into his belt. Worse than the bar owner getting his pistol free and firing, Mirabelle would be between the two of them. Caught in the cross fire, she wouldn't stand much of a chance.

Slocum tried to see if she was tied up. Her shoulders hunched forward, and she didn't move very much, as if her feet were bound together. A different approach to the camp was the only way to keep the woman out of the line of fire.

Working his way farther up the ravine, he came to a spot where it hardly reached his waist. He dropped forward and began a slow crawl back toward the camp. From this angle he saw Mirabelle's profile. She kept her head down, as if completely defeated. Had Malone or the others already had their way with her? That could explain her dejection.

Or it might be nothing more than resignation. They wouldn't keep her alive long when they figured out she didn't know where the stolen gold had been stashed.

Snow wet on his belly, he crawled closer. Something betrayed him. The crunching of the ice under his body might have alerted Beefsteak, or the man could have seen movement. Slocum crept through low bushes already turned brown and sere in anticipation of real winter storms.

Beefsteak dropped his plate and fork and grabbed for his six-shooter.

"You're a dead man if you haul that iron out," Slocum said. He punctuated his prediction by drawing back the hammer of his Colt. The metallic click sounded like a drumbeat in the sudden silence.

Everything froze. Beefsteak didn't move a muscle. Mirabelle was motionless, not even turning in his direction to see her rescuer.

"You got me, Slocum," Beefsteak said, raising his hands. "You gun down Willingham and his deputies, too?"

"One of 'em won't share in the gold," Slocum said. "Willingham and the other one with him are likely about back to Grizzly Flats by now." He doubted the marshal would give up quickly or easily. If he found the trail Slocum had left entering the canyon, he could mistake it in the dark for hoofprints leading away. That would keep him and his deputy busy for hours.

Willingham might not even find his way back to the camp and decide to stay on the trail all night long. However it worked out, the other two outlaws weren't a factor.

"Get to your feet," Slocum said.

As Malone obeyed, he also started to reach for his six-shooter, then stopped when he saw that Slocum's aim never wavered.

"You're right good with that smoke wagon, Slocum. I never seen you use it before you killed Eckerly. Didn't think you was mixed up in this."

"You just thought there'd be one less split for the gold," Slocum said, advancing.

"Something like that. Not sure when I figured you were in cahoots with her." He glanced in Mirabelle's direction. The woman had lifted her head, looking at Malone and not Slocum.

"Were you the one that beat me up after the funeral?"

"Not proud of all I've done, but can't say I regret it none, especially now. But Willingham is the one who takes the real pleasure in hurtin' folks."

"He killed Sennick and my Ike," Mirabelle said, finally finding her voice. "The marshal. Beefsteak here said so."

"Doesn't matter who did the killing or the raping or torturing. You're all guilty as sin." Slocum moved around to keep a good line of fire that avoided Mirabelle.

"If you'd meant to gun me down, you'd've done it by now. You gonna turn me over to the law?" This made Malone laugh uproariously.

Truth was, Slocum hadn't decided what to do with the gang. Three were dead, but he didn't gun men in cold blood, even if they deserved it. Malone, Willingham, and the deputy certainly did, but it was one thing to kill a man in a gunfight and another to back shoot or cut down an unarmed man.

"Take his gun, Mirabelle," Slocum said. "Be real careful when you do."

"What are you going to do, John?"

"You want to kill him, you can go ahead and do it. You got the grievance with him and the other two."

"All right," she said.

Mirabelle stood and reached out, small hand curling around the butt of the heavy pistol thrust into the man's belt. She tugged it out, almost dropped it, then hefted it in both hands.

"Suppose we ought to tie him up and—"

Slocum found himself staring down the gun barrel. Mirabelle had him dead to rights.

"Drop your gun, John," she said. "Drop it or I drop you."

"Don't think she won't do it neither," Malone said, laughing heartily. "She's a pretty damn good shot."

A thousand things ran through his head. None of the plans ended with him coming out alive. He dropped his six-gun.

"That's smart, Slocum, real smart," Malone said. He didn't move.

"Step away from your gun," Mirabelle said.

"The two of you have thrown in together?" Slocum wasn't

sure why this came as a surprise. As much as Mirabelle talked about how she had loved her husband, she had changed the longer they hunted for the gold until she shot and killed Smith without any qualms. And the dynamite she had rolled into the mine hadn't been a way of saving Slocum—it had been meant to seal him permanently in the shaft.

"Go on, honey chile, shoot him," Beefsteak said.

"No, he knows where the gold is. That's why he came back out here. There's no other reason."

In her head, she couldn't understand he had come to save her from the gang that had murdered her husband and friends. And maybe she was right. Slocum had certainly come hunting the gold, but if he had been only after the treasure from the train robbery, he wouldn't be staring down the barrel of a six-gun now.

Slocum said nothing, realizing his life hung by a slender thread. If Mirabelle thought he didn't know where the gold was, she would kill him out of hand.

"When did you two throw in together?" he asked.

"We came to a meeting of the minds," Beefsteak said, reaching down and taking Slocum's Colt off the ground. He began polishing off the mud. "As we was ridin' out into the mountains, we figgered out we worked better together than apart."

"You going to double-cross Willingham?"

From the smirk on Malone's lips, Slocum knew the answer without the saloon owner answering.

"I been lookin' for a fine woman like Mirabelle for a mighty long time. Not a whole lot to choose from in Grizzly Flats," the man said. "There's them whores, of course, but what fun is it if you have to pay for what you get?"

"You'll pay, one way or the other," Slocum said.

Beefsteak laughed and shook his head.

"Slocum, you ain't gonna drive a wedge 'tween me and this fine lady."

"Where's the gold, John?" The pistol never wavered in

her hands. "I'll count to five, then kill you if you haven't told me."

"Doesn't seem I have a whole lot of choice," Slocum said. "But if I do tell you, you're going to kill me anyway."

"Now, why'd you think that, Slocum? We're honest thieves. We keep our word. You tell her and you kin ride on off."

"Without the gold," Slocum said.

"You're not dumb, Slocum. Of course without the gold. But you ride off astride the saddle, not draped over it on your way to the cemetery."

Slocum knew his first thought was right. When he told these two his guess as to the gold's hiding place, he was a goner.

"One."

And if he didn't tell them now, Mirabelle was going to shoot him.

"Two." She sighted down the barrel. The muzzle looked big enough to reach down with his hand. The blunt noses of the bullets showed on either side of the pistol frame.

"Three."

Slocum's mind locked up.

"Four." Mirabelle's hand trembled now as her finger squeezed back on the trigger. Malone stood to one side, his hand on the butt of Slocum's pistol. If she missed, he wouldn't.

"Five."

"Wait!" Slocum held up his hand, as if to brush away the bullet that was sure to come whistling toward him. "I can't tell you. You'd never find it, but I can show you."

Malone chuckled and said, "You are a caution, Slocum. I wondered what you'd say to keep from gettin' yer damn fool head blowed off."

"Tell me now," Mirabelle said.

"Now, honey, don't go gettin' an itchy trigger finger. There'll be plenty of time for you to shoot him if he's lyin' or tries to double-cross us."

"I go free if I show you?" Slocum had to play along. Malone wouldn't buy his act but Mirabelle might. If he kept the two at loggerheads, he stood a better chance of getting away.

"That's what I tole you, Slocum. I'm not a man who goes back on my word. You worked for me for a couple weeks, so you know."

"You swear on the Damned Shame?"

"What?" For a moment, Beefsteak Malone stared at him in disbelief. Then he said, "You think that's the only thing I hold holy? Well, sir, you're damned right! I swear on my saloon that ever'thing I promised will be kept."

Slocum almost asked for Mirabelle to make a similar promise, then knew Malone would never allow it. She was his ace in the hole. If—when—it came down to finding the stolen gold, the saloon owner would let Mirabelle do the dirty work. Not that Malone would lose any sleep over a broken promise to a dead man.

"I'll tie him up, darlin', while you keep him covered."

Beefsteak took special glee in securing Slocum's hands behind him, then shoved him down near the fire.

"That'll keep you from freezin' in the dark. Me, I got my own personal bed warmer."

"Tie his feet, too," Mirabelle said. "He's a slippery one."

"You are the smart one here," Beefsteak said, doing as Mirabelle ordered. Only when he had finished did she allow him to take his six-shooter back.

Slocum watched as the pair curled up together under a single blanket, then tried not to pay a whole lot of attention to the undulations under the blanket or the sounds they made.

All he could think of as the fire and the passion died was how he was going to save his own neck come sunup. Slocum couldn't see a path that didn't lead to a grave for him.

19

"You think he's dead?" Mirabelle's soft voice carried just enough for Slocum to hear. He came awake, strained against the ropes around his wrists and legs, and turned toward the embers in the fire pit. Malone hadn't done much of a job keeping the fire burning, and Slocum was nigh on frozen.

"What's that, honey chile?"

"That fool Willingham," Mirabelle said. "Him and his deputy dead?"

"Cain't rightly say." Malone half turned and gave her a kiss. They had kept each other warm throughout the night.

Slocum decided he was as well off being half-frozen as sharing a blanket with Mirabelle. Better to find a snake and curl up with it. She was quite the murderer now, not caring if she shot men in the back or blew them up in a mine, and there she was sharing a blanket with the man who might have killed her husband and the rest of the party. Slocum never knew Lucas Sennick or Terrence or Isaac Comstock, but their greed wasn't as murderous as Beefsteak Malone's.

They had taken advantage of information and struck out

to find stolen gold. The railroad company had already soaked up the loss and hadn't gone belly up as a result. Why shouldn't whoever found the stolen money keep it? In Slocum's eyes, what Comstock and the others had tried was no different from Smith and Bertram eking out a pitiful existence in their gold mine. They knew the risks, they took them, and if they profited a little, that was all right. If they hit the mother lode, that was even better.

"Stop it," Mirabelle said, pushing him away. "It's danged near sunrise. We got to find the gold."

"Especially if Willingham ain't dead?"

"You want to share with that good-for-nothing marshal? I don't."

"He was the one what killed your hubby," Malone said.

Slocum couldn't tell if the man was lying or just toying with her. If he riled her enough, he might have one fewer partner once the gold was found.

And that presented Slocum with a dilemma. If he told them what he suspected, they'd kill him. He had to lead them on a wild-goose chase until he could get free. It mattered less to him now if he found the gold than it did getting away from Grizzly Flats alive. These hills already had been the scene of a terrible massacre. Adding his body to the list wasn't anything he cared to ponder.

It would be a hard row to hoe. He'd have to keep them confident he knew where the gold was, yet never—quite—find it. Considering how antsy Mirabelle was, he doubted he had longer than noon before she tired of him leading them around and just killed him. Malone might be a tad more tolerant, but Slocum wasn't going to bet on it. Not when it was his life on the line.

Twisting, he tried to get the ropes off his wrists enough to slide his hands through the loops. Beefsteak must have been a cowboy used to hog-tying calves. The rope had remained secure and the knot refused to budge, no matter how Slocum had tried to free himself all night long.

"We have time for some coffee?"

Slocum looked up. Malone towered over him, then bent and stirred the ashes. A few dried leaves caused a spark to fly, then he added a few twigs. In less than a minute the fire was roaring hot.

"Suppose so, but don't take long. And don't give him any," Mirabelle said.

"Why would I? It'd just be a waste." Malone laughed.

"So you're going to shoot me out of hand?" Slocum looked up.

"Only if you don't locate the gold pronto." Malone looked around, scanning the canyon mouths for any sign of the marshal and the deputy.

"What if I said the way lies down that canyon?" Slocum lifted his chin Navajo style to point where Beefsteak had been searching for Willingham.

"Then we go there, only if it ain't right, you don't get to come back here to camp. Not for dinner, not for a cup of this fine coffee Mira's fixed, not for nuthin'."

Slocum fell silent. He had less than ten minutes to silently strain at the ropes before Malone picked him up, threw him over his shoulder, and set off to track back in the snow to where Slocum had left his horse. The animal snorted in disgust at such mistreatment but otherwise looked none the worse for spending the night without a barn or fire. The saddle and blanket had probably kept the horse alive, trapping its body heat.

"Up you go," Malone said, slinging Slocum aloft. He grunted as he fell belly down over the saddle. A hiss of steel slicing through rope freed his legs. The saloon owner righted Slocum in the saddle, then looked at him. "You play fair or I set you up there backwards. No man's gonna get far tryin' to escape settin' backwards on a horse."

"I won't try."

"Damned if I don't believe you, Slocum." Beefsteak led the horse with Slocum astride back to the campfire, where

Mirabelle had already saddled their horses and waited impatiently.

"Where to?" she demanded.

"Looking for three rock spires. You remember how Smith drew them in the dust before you killed him?"

Slocum saw Beefsteak Malone straighten as he heard this. Mirabelle hadn't shared her bloodthirstier moments with him. The more Slocum could do to spin contention between them, the longer he was going to be alive.

"He was plumb loco from livin' alone," she said.

"I found them. Across this meadow, then head north."

"Let's ride!" Beefsteak let out a whoop and trotted off, leaving Mirabelle to lead Slocum's horse.

"He'll gun you down like he did Ike and the others," Slocum said.

"No, he won't. The big fool's in love with me."

Slocum couldn't tell if Mirabelle believed that or wanted to believe it.

"We're goin' over to Frisco. I know some fine places where Ike couldn't never take me 'cuz we didn't have money. Beefsteak's gonna take me to the Union Club. We're gonna get all gussied up in fine store-bought clothes and arrive in a carriage pulled by two white horses and then we're gonna hobnob with them rich folk, 'cuz we're gonna be rich."

Malone rode far ahead, champing at the bit as much as Mirabelle, but the woman kept on with her highfalutin dreams of what she and Malone would do once they got rich. Slocum couldn't tell why she went on like this because he heard just a hint of something more in her voice.

Greed.

An hour's ride took them to a canyon that looked familiar, even with a fresh dusting of snow on the rocks. Slocum led them down this canyon and then up a branching one, then rocked back to stop his horse. Smack dab ahead were the three rocky spires.

"That the rocks you said the miner told you about?"

Malone asked. He frowned a little. "Why'd he tell you and not come fer the gold himself? He'd been out here plenty long enough to hunt."

"He had old-fashioned ways," Slocum said. "He wanted to earn what he made."

Malone laughed and said, "Now we're different, aren't we, Slocum? Me and you? We don't mind a bit o' stealin'."

"Quit yakking," Mirabelle snapped. "There's the three stone towers. Don't much look like Smith scratched in the dirt, but you say that's what we're huntin', then that's where we are. Where's the cave?"

Slocum rode toward the cave where he had found the ten coins earlier. His time was running out fast. He needed to come up with a way of staying alive—but he couldn't think of anything.

As he let his horse pick its way through the icy rocks, he used his numbed fingers to pull his coat around. Working his fingers up under it, he felt the pocket where he had put the gold coins he'd found before. Worrying at a seam, he got a small hole started. By the time they reached the cave, he had torn the seam open enough to get out a half dozen of the twenty-dollar gold pieces.

"Come on down and show us." Beefsteak reached up, grabbed the front of Slocum's coat, and heaved.

Slocum flew through the air and landed so hard it jarred his teeth. Dazed, he was in no condition to fight as Malone pulled him to his feet and shoved him into the cave. Using the grogginess as a cover, Slocum crashed into one wall, rebounded, and fell toward the other, spinning as he fell so he landed on his side.

The gold coins he'd taken from his pocket dropped to the dirt floor. As Malone pulled him upright, he swept as much of the dirt and debris as he could over the coins to hide them.

"You sure this is the place?" Mirabelle had Slocum's Colt aimed at his forehead. "If you're lyin', John, this will be your tomb."

"Around," he said, feigning more confusion than he felt. "Search all the way back. There's plenty around."

"Now don't go runnin' off," Beefsteak said, wagging his finger in Slocum's face. "I don't need no target practice."

He and Mirabelle went toward the distant back of the cave. A lucifer exploded into light. Malone held it out and they began looking in every cranny they could for the gold. As they hunted, Slocum worked his ropes against a sharp rock in the cave wall. He became frantic to shred the rope as the two worked their way back toward him more rapidly than he'd hoped.

"We ain't findin' the gold, Slocum. I'm thinkin' my honey chile here's gonna get to shoot you."

Slocum rolled away from the spot where he had worked on the ropes and left the coins.

"Search harder," he said. "What I saw was on the floor."

He found another spot with a sharpened rock. He stopped sawing and began pressing the rope hard into the rock. Strand after strand popped. Blood trickled down into the palms of his hands, making them almost useless to grip anything. All he saw around him as a weapon was a small rock the size of his fist. Even if Mirabelle ventured too close and he recovered his six-shooter, he doubted he would be able to fire it accurately, not with his hands in such bad shape.

"There's nuthin' here," Beefsteak said.

But Mirabelle had stopped near the place where Slocum had salted the mine with the coins. She shuffled her foot about, then dived down, scrabbling in the dirt like a gopher digging a burrow. A dust cloud rose. Slocum took the chance to rub his wrists and get some feeling back into his swollen hands. Blood smeared his fingers and then he quickly stopped and pretended once more to be tied up when the dust cloud was swept out of the cave by a sudden gust of wind.

Beefsteak stood, slightly bent over because of the low

ceiling, looking intently at him. Then he began sifting through the dust beside Mirabelle. Within seconds they both had a couple gold coins.

"You weren't lyin', Slocum," the man said, shaking his head in wonder.

"There's got to be more," Mirabelle said. "We got to dig!" She held out three coins. Beefsteak Malone had two. Slocum didn't know how many he had dropped. His hands had barely been agile enough to rip the coat pocket.

"Where?" Beefsteak looked around. "That's solid rock floor. The dust is only an inch thick at most."

"There's a crevice in the back of the cave," Slocum said. "Big enough for a leather bag to get crammed down out of sight."

Both of them lit out like he'd set fire to their boots. Pushing and complaining, they began examining each crack in the rock, no matter how small. Slocum held his breath, then waited for the flare of another lucifer. When it came, he knew they'd both be blinded for a few seconds.

He shot to his feet at the burst of light. Keeping low, trying not to make any sound, he stumbled from the cave mouth and looked for his horse.

Instead of his horse, he found himself staring down the wrong end of a gun barrel.

"Now, where do you think you're goin', Slocum?" Marshal Willingham asked.

Slocum raised his hands in surrender.

20

"Never thought I'd run into you again, Slocum," the marshal said.

"Where's your deputy?" Slocum looked around, hoping for even a hint of distraction that would let him get away.

The mountaintops were already clouded over, and the wind whipping into the cave from the direction of the triple peaks tore at Slocum's face. The urge to go for his six-shooter was overwhelming, but it would do him no good. Mirabelle had the Colt Navy.

"Him? Well, now, let's just say that he fell a damned far ways to his death."

"You find the gold?" Slocum still held out a sliver of hope to distract Willingham, but it wasn't working. Worse, he heard footsteps from behind.

Both Malone and Mirabelle came from the cave.

"What do we have here? You caught this varmint just in time, Will," Beefsteak said. "We turned our backs on him for a second, and look what he tried to up and do."

"You didn't let him go for the pleasure of huntin' him down and then killin' him?"

"Not like the others this time, Will, no, sir, not at all."

"They found the gold in the cave," Slocum said, still angling for an edge.

The roar of Malone's six-shooter in his ear left him with a headache and a ringing that stole away his hearing for a few seconds. He looked over his shoulder. Malone had aimed and fired directly into the marshal's badge. For his part, Willingham simply sat, a confused look on his face. Then he died.

"Always knew Will wore that star for a reason. Made a damned fine target," Malone said.

"He said his deputy was coming anytime now. When he hears the gunfire, he'll—"

"Do no such thing. I overheard my dearly departed friend Will say that he'd killed his deputy for me. That was real thoughty of him 'cuz it saved me the ammo," Malone said, laughing.

Slocum edged away from the saloon owner toward the marshal's body. Willingham had dropped his six-shooter, but it was out of reach. Slocum needed something more to distract Malone if he had any hope of getting it.

"You ain't got a snowball's chance in hell of gettin' to his gun 'fore I shoot, Slocum," Malone said, swinging his pistol around to center on Slocum's chest.

A sudden gust of wind blew a few snowflakes into Malone's face. Slocum dived for the marshal's six-gun as a loud report filled the canyon with new echoes. He skidded on his belly, sure a second shot would come after the first miss. Scrambling, he reached for the gun, then froze.

Beefsteak Malone still stood, but his face had gone flaccid. His jaw dropped, as if he tried to say something. He failed. Like a tree toppled in the forest, he fell forward stiff as a board. Immediately behind him, Mirabelle held Slocum's pistol. The brisk wind had whipped away the smoke from the muzzle, but there was no doubt she had shot Malone in the back.

"You keep away from that there gun, John," she said, motioning for him to move back.

"You want the gold all for yourself?"

"Why not? These bastards killed Ike and the others. What do I owe them?"

"You were talking about going to San Francisco and hobnobbing in high society with Malone."

"I can do it on my own. I can have my pick of them eligible men with enough money in my hands." She motioned him back into the cave. He couldn't get close enough to jump her; Mirabelle was coldly methodical now as she picked up both Willingham's and Malone's six-shooters.

Then she riffled through Malone's pockets and pulled out the two twenty-dollar gold pieces he had found.

Slocum began to sweat in spite of the sudden drop in temperature. The clouds were turning leaden with the promise of a new snowstorm, and the wind chilled his body. The idea that Mirabelle would kill him as ruthlessly as she had Malone chilled his soul. Although he wasn't one to dwell on the subject, this wasn't the way he had ever thought he would die.

"We didn't find the stash. Show me that crevice where you say the bag's jammed down."

"We were good together," Slocum lied. "We can split the gold. I know a lot of places in San Francisco where—"

"Shut up," she said in a voice lacking any emotion. That told Slocum more about his fate than if she had screamed at him. Mirabelle Comstock had turned into a stone killer and wouldn't likely ever so much as think of him once she rode away.

Only Slocum knew she would be thinking of him. Thinking and cursing his name because there wasn't any gold to find.

"Right back where you and Beefsteak looked," Slocum said.

"We searched every inch of the cave."

"Not by the spot where you found the coins," Slocum said. He moved to where he had dropped the few coins.

Reaching into his coat pocket, he felt two remaining gold pieces. He palmed them, then shoved his hand into a shallow crevice, pretended to fish around, and then let out a yelp of glee.

"Look what I found. The bag broke and the coins are at the bottom." He held out the two gleaming coins.

This was all the opening he needed. Mirabelle focused entirely on the new find and reached for them. He dropped the coins. Her eyes followed the spinning disks to the cave floor—and Slocum grabbed for his six-gun. With a hard yank, he pried it from her fingers and stepped away to get the drop on her.

His boot heel caught on a rock, and he sat hard. The gun discharged and brought down a cascade of rock and dirt from above. By the time he could see through the dusty brown veil, Mirabelle had fled. Grunting with effort, he got to his feet and cautiously peered out of the cave mouth. He had saved his own life. It would be foolish to let her ambush him now.

For a moment, Slocum couldn't decide what was different. Then it came to him. Willingham's horse was gone. Mirabelle had rushed from the cave, mounted, and ridden off. The wind's whine had muffled her retreat. Slocum ventured farther out and looked down the valley to see her hunched over the horse's neck, forcing as much speed from it as she could.

"Good riddance," Slocum said, sliding his Colt back into the holster. It gave a familiar, comforting weight to his left hip.

He returned to the cave, found the two coins he'd used as bait, and put them in his other coat pocket, the one without a hole in the bottom. What had happened to rest of the twenty-dollar gold pieces was a poser. He was happy to be ahead any amount of money.

He went back out, fetched his and the other two horses, then rode into the growing storm. He ought to find shelter to ride it out, but something more drove him. There'd be time later if he didn't find the real hiding place. He stopped in the middle of the canyon and looked out. A meadow stretched toward the three peaks. He pursed his lips as he thought on how train robbers would hide their ill-gotten gains. The first place they found might not be good enough.

That was about in a straight line from the leftmost peak. Slocum turned in the saddle and followed the line to the cave where he'd found the coins. Likely, there hadn't been an adequate hiding place in that cave. So where would they go? The central peak kept drawing his eye. Following it back down into the canyon took him past the hill where the first cave had yielded the handful of gold to a pile of rocks near the canyon wall, where it bent at an angle to the northeast.

The right-hand peak didn't offer anything he could see to guide a treasure hunter. He led his horses toward the spot on the rocky wall indicated by the center peak, the wind cutting at his back. The storm was building, but its full fury wouldn't seize the land for another hour or two.

Slocum rode directly to the rocks he had singled out as his best bet. Frantic train robbers might have tucked their gold under a loose stone. Then he saw a sandy pit protected on two sides by towering rocks. One way was open and a dark hole in the canyon wall gave what Slocum would consider a decent hiding place.

He left his horses in the sandy pit, glad that the rocks protected them from the biting wind. Hand on his pistol, less wary of snakes in this cold than he was of other varmints, he went into the cave. The heavy musk smell told him this had been a den for coyotes or wolves. He drew his six-shooter and inched forward. The carcass of a medium-sized timber wolf showed why the others had abandoned this fine shelter.

Without a lot more work than he wanted to expend, there

was no way to tell if the wolf had been shot or had died of some other cause. Its skull was shattered, but the reason was long hidden by insects and smaller scavengers making off with tasty bits of the carcass.

He dragged a lucifer across the rocky wall and held it high as it flared. His eyes widened when he saw scratches on the back wall that looked like someone's initials. Slocum wished he had learned the train robbers' names, then he decided it didn't matter. This wasn't a grave. It was a repository for wealth.

Stolen wealth.

Digging furiously, he found that the floor was less rock and more dirt for a few inches. When he hit solid rock, he also noticed a hole in the floor had been filled with dirt. Working his fingers down, he tensed when he touched leather. He dug a bit more, snared a leather thong, and yanked. The bag resisted his pull. He worked away more of the dirt and gravel, then hefted the bag. It sagged to the floor, heavy with gold coins.

Slocum didn't try to slow the frenzied beating of his heart. There were thousands of dollars in gold coins in the bag. For the first time he understood why so many people had wanted to recover the loot—and why so many had died.

He lifted the bag with both hands and carried it out to the sandy spit. To keep the weight from being too onerous, he split the coins between his saddlebags and those on what had been Beefsteak's horse. For a moment he stood and stared at how the horses' hindquarters sagged just a little under the weight.

Then the wind slipping noisily through the rocks around him took a pause, and he heard another sound.

"You didn't think I'd let you keep it all, did you, John? That other cave wasn't right. This was."

He half turned to hide his right hand as he reached for his six-shooter.

A shot rang out, louder than anything he had ever heard

in his life. The report was trapped in the ring of rocks and bounced around. More than this, his racing heart filled his ears with the rush of his own blood.

He didn't draw, though. Mirabelle Comstock lay face-down on the ground, Malone's gun by her left hand and Willingham's clutched in her right. He saw the slowly spreading circle of blood on the back of her head. Her mousy brown hair matted quickly and soaked up what leaked from her brain.

"Aren't you going to give me a proper greeting?"

"Hello, Madeleine," he said. "What brings you out on a stormy day like this?"

"Other than saving your worthless hide? Oh, I decided Grizzly Flats and I needed to part company. I thought it might be fun for us to ride together for a while." The red-head blew away smoke still curling from the muzzle of her derringer and tucked it into a small beaded handbag. She looked as if she had dressed for a soiree and not the trail. "You don't like my clothes? I can take them off."

"I owe you," he said.

"Don't flatter yourself, Mr. Slocum. I enjoyed our time together and hope we share much more, but you owe me nothing."

"Nothing?"

"Nothing," she said.

"Even if I found a cave loaded with gold?" He watched her reaction closely.

"What do I care about that, even if you did? But you men are such liars. It doesn't take a big poke to impress a lady." Her eyes went to his crotch. "Besides, you have already impressed me." She stepped over Mirabelle and came forward to give him a proper kiss.

"We can make a few miles away from here before the storm hits," Slocum said, breaking off the kiss.

"I found an abandoned shack as I followed your trail. Oh, don't look so surprised. I have many skills, and tracking is just one of them. I was a stage actress before I was a school-marm, you know."

"I didn't," he said. "Are you acting now?"

"I was thinking more about teaching you a few things." She spun away and worked futilely to tuck her copper hair under her hat. The wind worked faster than she did and she finally gave up. "I'm heading to San Francisco. If you're going that way, you can ride with me."

"If I'm not?" Slocum asked.

"That would be such a shame, but as I said, I can fend for myself, thank you."

"Since you're going my way, I'll go with you," Slocum said, grinning. He led his small remuda back into the wind as Madeleine followed.

It wasn't until they reached San Francisco that he told Madeleine about the gold. As he'd hoped, it didn't change anything between them.